ELYON

LOST BOOK 6

TED DEKKER
AND
KACI HILL

THOMAS NELSON
Since 1798

NASHVILLE DALLAS MEXICO CITY RIO DE JANEIRO

Published in Nashville, Tennessee, by Thomas Nelson. Thomas Nelson is a registered trademark of Thomas Nelson, Inc.

Published in association with Thomas Nelson and Creative Trust, Inc., 5141 Virginia Way, Suite 320, Brentwood, TN 37027.

Thomas Nelson books may be purchased in bulk for educational, business, fund-raising, or sales promotional use. For information, please e-mail SpecialMarkets@ThomasNelson.com.

Page design by Casey Hooper
Map design by Chris Ward

ISBN 978-1-59554-684-5 (TP)

Library of Congress Cataloging-in-Publication Data

Dekker, Ted, 1962–
Elyon / Ted Dekker and Kaci Hill.
p. cm. — (Lost books ; bk. 7)
"A Lost Book."
Summary: The Chosen Ones need Elyon's grace to face their greatest threat yet, but Darsal is torn between her new mission, trying to love the Horde as Elyon asked her to, and her original one, especially now that Johnis and Silvie no longer seem to be on her side.
ISBN 978-1-59554-374-5 (hardcover)
[1. Fantasy. 2. Christian life—Fiction.] I. Hill, Kaci. II. Title.
PZ7.D3684Ely 2009
[Fic]—dc22 2009007891a

Printed in the United States of America
10 11 12 13 14 RRD 7 6 5 4 3 2

BEGINNINGS

Our story begins in a world totally like our own, yet completely different. What once happened seems to be repeating itself two thousand years later.

Twenty years have passed since the lush, colored forests were turned into desert by Teeleh, enemy of Elyon and vilest of all creatures. Evil now rules the land and shows itself as a painful, scaly disease that covers the flesh of the Horde.

The powerful green waters, once precious to Elyon, vanished from the earth. Those few who chose to follow the ways of Elyon bathed once daily in those waters to cleanse their skin of the scabbing disease. For thirteen years, the number of their sworn enemy, the Horde, grew, and the Forest Guard was severely diminished by war, forcing Thomas, supreme commander, to lower the army's recruitment age to sixteen. A thousand young recruits showed themselves worthy and served in the Forest Guard.

From among the thousand, four young fighters—Johnis, Silvie, Billos, and Darsal—were handpicked by Thomas to lead.

Unbeknownst to Thomas, the four heroes were also chosen by the legendary white Roush, guardians of all that is good, for a far greater mission, and were forbidden to tell a soul. Braving terrible battles, crushing defeat, capture, death, and betrayal, they pursued their quest to find the seven original Books of History, a mission that took them from one reality into another.

From their world to the histories, two thousand years into their past, into a city known as Las Vegas, their journey ended deep in the mountains of Romania. On the day after their great victory, having secured all seven books—thereby foiling the plans of the Dark One, who would use the books to destroy humankind—they left our world to return to Thomas and the Forest Guard, two thousand years from now.

But five years have passed since they left their home in the distant future. The world they once knew has changed in favor of their sworn enemy, the Horde. Qurong now rules the city. He has a new high priest—Sucrow, a ruthless servant of Teeleh—to replace Ciphus, who killed Witch. He also has a new general by the name of Marak, sworn to kill every albino on the face of the earth.

Forced to flee the city, Darsal, Johnis, and Silvie have become separated. Worse, Elyon's water, once green, is now red and has apparently lost its healing properties. Johnis and Silvie are soon consumed by the scabbing disease.

To further complicate matters, the Shataiki have mated with some of the Horde, creating a strange race of predatory creatures known as the Leedhan. Insanely jealous of the Leedhan's half-human appearance, Teeleh banished them to the far side of a great river. Outcast and despised, the Leedhan are thought to be gone forever.

But one of them, their embittered queen, named Shaeda, has returned. She has come to seize control of the Horde, and to overthrow Teeleh himself. To do so she needs a human, and she has chosen none other than Johnis as her agent for revenge.

Shaeda seduced Johnis and has fully possessed him. Completely deceived, both Johnis and Silvie have made an alliance with the priest Sucrow with promises of destroying Thomas Hunter and the Circle in three days. But to do so they must acquire a legendary amulet that gives its owner control over the Shataiki.

Meanwhile, Darsal has encountered a different fate. She's discovered the secret of the new red waters—that drowning in its depths heals one of the scabbing disease. Having drowned in the red waters, Darsal has accepted a mission from Elyon: to return to the Horde . . . and love them.

Now our three fallen heroes—Darsal, Johnis, and Silvie—find themselves pitted against each other while the world awaits its fate.

ONE

Marak of Southern, Qurong's general over all the Horde army, paced inside one of the bunk rooms reserved for the officers. Two narrow beds stacked on top of each other jutted out of each wall. No windows. Just a torch stand and the candles on his desk. Behind him was a narrow shelf of books.

His captain and best friend, Cassak, was taking too long to bring in the prisoners. He had said he would be here by now. Marak's patience was running out.

"Where is he?" Marak grumbled to himself, storming over to the two open books on the desk. One had once belonged to the long-gone general Martyn, who'd trained him; and the other, to his dead betrothed, Rona.

How, in Teeleh's name, had everything gone wrong in a week? He was a general, for goodness' sake, respected and trusted and feared. He'd been a good man with a loyal brother and a soon-to-be wife.

And now . . .

General Marak had sequestered himself in the officers' hall at the north end of Middle, with fifty warriors standing guard. For two days they had roasted in the hot sun, choosing loyalty to their general over the orders of the Dark Priest. And for two days all of Middle remained tense, caught in the battle lines drawn between High Priest Sucrow and Marak.

Marak took a long swig of his drink and continued his trek around the room. The meal his slave had brought him earlier sat untouched on the table. He couldn't eat; his stomach felt as if it were full of knives.

He went to the door and swung it open. "Is Darsal here yet?"

"No, sir," the warrior replied, falling into his salute. "We've not yet seen—"

"Find her."

"My lord—"

"Find her!" Marak shut the door and went back to his inner tirade. This was a mistake. All of it. He'd had everything under control a week ago. At least, as much as the mess left by his predecessor allowed.

In less than a week, the priest had undone everything Marak had built, all in a bizarre sense of revenge and power play. Marak hadn't wanted to defy Qurong—and technically he hadn't. He had no reason to. But a series of events had led him to defy the

Dark Priest and sequester himself in the officers' quarters. Now Qurong, the supreme commander, must hear him out on the absurd notion of a general taking orders from a priest. He had to.

Knotting his fist and glowering at the cold plate of food, he reviewed this plunge into dishonor.

First, upon gaining rank over Marak, Sucrow had ordered him to execute his own family—all albinos. Marak had stalled as long as possible, but Sucrow was powermongering.

Marak's jaw tensed at that thought. It'd been some time since he'd given the order and stood by as Cassak administered the hideous potion—Marak's albino-killing concoction called the Desecration—to his family. His brother.

He whirled around to the door and thrust his head out again. "Why are you still standing there?" he barked at the guard. "Did you find her?"

"The albino is still out on your previous orders, General," the guard replied cautiously. "I've sent a scout for her."

"Good." Again Marak turned back to his predicament. Where was he . . . ? Oh, right. His second problem. Sucrow had struck a deal with this Josef character from the backside of the desert, who claimed to have a better, faster way of killing off the albinos: a magic amulet made of Leedhan magic—whatever that was—that would give control over the mythical Shataiki and command them to wipe out the blight that is the albinos.

Marak had dismissed the idea. Sucrow had not.

Which led him to his third problem: Sucrow had taken Josef

and Arya and had gone after the amulet without him. Immediately upon learning this, Marak sent his captain, Cassak, after them. If Sucrow was so convinced and so willing to risk his life for this amulet, there had to be some merit to its power.

Acting upon Marak's order, Cassak had captured Josef and Arya and taken the amulet from them. The move had infuriated Sucrow, so Marak had moved into the officers' quarters, barred the windows, and set guards around the sundial for his and his prisoners' protection.

So here he was. For two days Sucrow had made no move, but that would not last.

So be it. Marak had the amulet and the two prisoners, Josef and Arya, in his custody. His slave, Darsal, knew them as Johnis of Middle and Silvie of Southern, but he did not. Whatever their reasons were, he would not yet let them know he had that information. A knock at the door snapped him out of his silent rant.

"Who is it?" he growled.

"Darsal. Let me in."

Darsal, his albino slave, had been in the cells the same night his family was executed and had spoken with them before their deaths. She wore his brother's Circle pendant around her neck, his gift to her. Marak wasn't sure why he'd spared her, but he had. Twice. Once that night, when she vowed to be his slave. The second time in a glen, shortly after Sucrow had ordered him to kill her and, to his horror, he found he could not.

This at least partly explained his rationale to sequester himself here in the officers' quarters. Qurong might not yet know Darsal was still alive despite Sucrow's orders. And Sucrow couldn't use her in his sadistic rites—or worse yet, kill her—if Marak still had her.

"Marak, are you going to let me in?" The knob was rattling. He quickly crossed the room to unhook the latch and swing the door open.

There she was. This albino slave, this woman . . . Darsal of the Far Northern Forest, who claimed to have crossed time and space through worn leather portals called the Books of History. She stood before him, arms crossed. Morst covered her exposed skin, and a blue veil wrapped around her head, covering her nose and mouth. Rich brown eyes watched him, noticeably frustrated.

"Thank you," she said. "You summoned me?" Their eyes met.

If he wasn't mistaken, he was falling in love with her. With an albino. This was most definitely a mistake.

He forgot what he'd summoned her for. He released a breath and worked the knot of frustration and anxiety back down into his belly.

"General." Darsal spoke softly, pulling him out of his thoughts. The citrus scent she wore drifted through the room.

Oh. Right. He was a general with a thousand problems to take care of. Unwilling to be caught in her warm gaze again, Marak stormed down the dark hall to the war room.

"Has Cassak arrived yet?" he asked her as he shoved the door open, not missing a step.

"Not yet," Darsal said, straightening the blue veil. She watched his irritated pacing, characteristic of the last several hours. He circled around the eight-foot oval table made of cherrywood. A green runner draped the width of the table, laid squarely beneath three copper candelabra. White pillars of wax flickered as curls of smoke drifted through the war room.

"He'll be here," Darsal said.

He tugged at the collar of his rust-colored tunic, sweaty and itchy, and turned toward the east-facing window he'd had Cassak's men bar and cover with a heavy crimson drape so no one could see in. Every window in the building had received the same treatment. The room was dark, but he couldn't very well light the torches without suffocating them all. Why Darsal would unnecessarily coat herself in morst, then drape a veil over her head in here, was beyond him.

Her fruity scent mingled with that of the candles.

"Relax, Marak. He'll be here."

Focus.

"He's certainly taking his time about it. Read the message again," he ordered, turning back to her.

"It hasn't changed, my *general*." Darsal quirked a brow, completely exasperated with him. Her veil slipped, revealing dark brown braids. "He'll be here with your amulet and your prisoners."

"Just read it. I don't have the patience for your obstinacy. Not today. Not when we're at the brink of a civil war and Sucrow is halfway to Qurong by now. If your so-called friends hadn't been so stupid—"

"It was the Throaters' fault, and you know it. Cassak said so himself."

"They were only out there because they're a bunch of superstitious religious idiots who convinced the priest one of his own myths might be true," he argued.

"Jordan believed Shataiki exist," Darsal pushed. Marak tensed. "And the Roush. And Elyon. Was your brother a fool, Marak?"

Marak scowled at her. "Jordan was mistaken on many things. That didn't make him a fool."

"Yet you call drowning foolish."

"Your persistence is aggravating."

She studied him. "You're missing the point of all of this, my general."

"What's that?" He almost regretted the question. He knew her answer.

"This is about—"

"Elyon. You keep saying that."

"More than that, Marak. I mean, yes. But you're still missing it. Elyon doesn't just love the Circle. He loves the Horde too. You. This is all about you and Elyon. That's why I'm here." She opened her arms wide, indicating the room. "All of this."

Marak started to protest but was interrupted by a knock at the door. Secretly he appreciated the diversion from her nonsense about being Elyon's emissary. "We don't have time for this. Who is it?" he growled, unwilling to open the door on a whim.

"A messenger from the captain, General!" a familiar voice called through the door. Cassak's favored scout.

Marak nodded at Darsal, who let the scout in. She'd taken to staying by the door, even so far as to sleep in front of the threshold at night. A curious thing.

The small warrior saluted and went to one knee. Marak bid him stand, then bellowed, "He's late."

"He was avoiding the Throaters," the scout explained. "He's bringing the prisoners from the southeast to avoid further confrontation with the rebels."

Marak queried him on Eram, the half-breed rebel, then came to his real question. "When will Cassak be here?"

"Shortly, sir. He's making sure the prisoners and the amulet are secure. He's already sent messages to the commanders so they can respond to the rebels accordingly."

"Tell me something," he asked the scout. "Were you there?"

"Yes, sir."

"Exactly what did you see?"

"Well, sir, it was just like the captain's report said."

"And no one would obey the captain?"

"Oh, *we* did, sir. We didn't kill any of them. Warryn and his men did the killing."

Marak bit back a comment. "What else? Cassak kept talking about black trees and clouds."

The scout didn't answer. He kept looking at Darsal. Staring. What was this scout looking at Darsal for?

"You have a problem, soldier?" Marak growled. He resisted the urge to jump between Darsal and the stupid scout and slice his head off.

The scout backed up. "No sir."

"Then answer the question." From what Marak had already gleaned from his scouts and an irritating message from Cassak, Josef wanted Sucrow's assistance—which meant Marak needed information. There was no way he was letting the priest race off with Marak's prisoners, much less in secrecy, with delusions of glory and self-aggrandizement in his head.

"Well, sir, it's just that no one's really sure what we saw."

Marak threw Darsal an over-the-shoulder glance.

"Were they furry?" Darsal interrupted, startling both Marak and the scout. She appeared beside him, so close he was drowning in her scent. A flash of heat shot up his arm where hers brushed his. "Black fur, leathery wings, red eyes. Do you remember that?"

"Albino," Marak warned, snapping his head around. But that was his mistake. Their eyes met . . .

He broke the gaze first.

Never again.

"Bring some water." Marak kept his voice even. Tried to calm it just a little.

She raised a brow. "It's . . . *water* you want?"

What business did she have bringing up the red lakes with Cassak's scout in the room? He answered slowly. "Not that water."

Darsal left without answering. Marak finished business with the scout and dismissed him. For the next few minutes he was alone. "Jordan," he muttered. "What I wouldn't give to fight this out with you right now."

"Marak." Darsal's voice startled him. He turned, and she offered him a bottle of water and a small scroll with Qurong's seal on it. "This just came."

"Read it." He drank greedily as she opened the message and scanned it.

"It's a summons to the palace. Qurong wants to know what happened out there."

"He should ask his bloody priest. My hands are tied."

"So get them untied."

Marak eyed Darsal as she took a swig of water.

"I'm just saying," she explained, "in less than a week, Sucrow started what you've spent a year and a half preventing." She read on, her voice suddenly tense. "It's about the expedition."

Marak didn't answer.

"I'm not Jordan, but I'll fight it out with you."

"You weren't supposed to hear that."

Darsal raised her gaze to him. Sighed. "Follow your heart, Marak."

His eyes narrowed. Now, that was a strange thing to say. "My heart?"

"That's what Thomas always said. Elyon speaks through the heart. Love." She touched his chest.

Marak frowned. Bit his tongue. Would his heart have killed his family or saved them? His heart was a black-riddled coward.

"Elyon's who got us into this mess."

A short commotion caught his attention. The pair listened, both reaching for blades on instinct, even though Darsal didn't have one. He then realized she had reached for one of his.

"Must be Cassak, finally," Marak growled.

"Try making an ally rather than an enemy of him," Darsal said. Marak eyed her. "Johnis, I mean."

Great. Now Darsal was playing games too.

"Why? Planning on drowning them as well?"

"I might be."

"I think not. You'll wait in the hall."

SUCROW SAT IN THE SHADOWS, MASKED BY CURLING SMOKE. Incense filled his nostrils. He knelt down on a silk cushion before the winged-serpent image of Teeleh and prayed for the success of the coming expedition, that their destruction of the albinos would find favor with him and be a fragrant offering to the Great One.

At last he lifted his forehead from the ground and sat straight on his knees, gazing up at the icon.

"My lord," one of his servants spoke from behind. Sucrow scowled. "Qurong sends for you and the general."

He paused. "Very well. Be gone."

Footsteps carried the informer away. Sucrow turned back to

Teeleh and repeated his petition. Breathing deeply, he entered his trance and embraced the vision that came to him. He stood before the altar and drank in the depths of what he knew to be his master's lair. As the room chilled, a low growl and acidic breath came over his shoulder. Sucrow didn't turn. A taloned claw traced his throat, cold and hard. Sinewy fingers touched his skin.

His master. The Great One. Teeleh.

"I do not care to be petitioned so that my servants might complain of their own failures, priest," his master warned. "And now this is what you will do: bring me the blood of the one long ago chosen, and ensure the medallion falls into your hands. I will not tolerate the vampiress any longer. The Leedhan must face penalty for her insolence."

Sucrow lifted his face, further exposing his throat to his master. "Lord?"

"Do not allow them to cross the river."

Confusion overtook him. But before he could ask, the chill seeped from the room, along with the presence.

"My lord . . . Warryn has returned."

Warryn, the foolish chieftain who had embarrassed him. A pebble in the shoe to be dealt with.

"Bring him in."

Warryn soon stood before Sucrow, who looked his wayward chieftain over, scrutinizing him. The chief serpent warrior had been tainted. Penalties were required. "An eye for an eye," wasn't that how the saying went? Sucrow would give Warryn's position to another, but he would also take Warryn's eye. A more formidable ally with a sense of duty and honor. If Marak could not be persuaded . . . his captain likely could.

The thought of an entire army of serpent warriors, all led by a chieftain and general who served the Great One with faithfulness . . .

"My lord . . ."

"Summon the officers," Sucrow ordered. "And you, Warryn, will at last be humiliated before your favorite captain." He sneered.

Warryn remained stoic. He bowed and left to retrieve the officers.

Sucrow looked through his library, seeking his book of incantations. Relighting the incense, he spoke a prayer to his master and bowed prostrate before Teeleh's image six times.

What Teeleh's intentions were, he didn't know. But that was not his place. Marak had the amulet, the young chosen one, and his arrogance. Soon all would be Sucrow's. Soon. Josef wouldn't even know what to do with such power.

"If Marak cannot be bought or intimidated, another must take his place," he said to himself.

Sucrow took a bird from its cage and put the tiny creature on the altar. Using a sharp blade with a heavily jeweled handle, he pierced the bird in its heart. Blood seeped out and around the small fowl, forming a pool on the altar. Sucrow slid the knife down the bird's chest, exposing its twitching organs. He withdrew a vial and mixed its contents into the bird's blood, mingling with the entrails, and read from the book the proper spell.

"Who shall succeed you, most foolish of generals, so lofty, so proud? From such great heights you have fallen, O infidel!"

Fog and haze slithered over the room like so many snakes. He breathed deep the pungent aroma and shut his eyes a moment . . . then opened them. Sucrow lifted his staff over the concoction and stirred the empty air until a greenish-red light appeared.

He used a bone to mix the blood and entrails, careful not to let the substance touch his skin. Sucrow's mantra continued. Teeleh's eyes formed in the shadows, glaring at him. He dipped his head.

"Tell me, my seeing eye, my great wonder from the sky, who shall succeed our general who must die?"

The eyes swelled, growing together into a single, enormous orb that opened into a reddish mirror, a pool's reflection in midair. Soon a face appeared, one in desert tans and browns who stood at his general's side.

"Ah, Captain, so you are the next in line." Sucrow chuckled, watching in the mirror as Cassak led the prisoners to their captor.

He stirred the entrails again.

A stream of greenish-yellow light drifted from the end of his staff. It formed a spiral, coming ever closer to the captain's image. The light snaked around and grew brighter. It burst into a thousand stars, blinding him for a moment.

Then a glittering blue star appeared in his palm, resting on a short cord.

Of course, the good captain would never willingly fall in league with his general's enemy. But Sucrow had already compromised him once during the ordeal regarding Jordan and Rona. Still, he could not afford for anything to go wrong.

Sucrow raised his staff and spun it, reciting another incantation, ignoring the pain that always came with transformation. His body screamed as it twisted, bent, and stretched into the form he desired.

He took a deep breath and waited. It was finished. He walked to the ornate mirror, framed by wooden snakes, and looked into the glass. A young scout greeted his reflection. Good.

He changed his clothes and stuffed them in a bag over his shoulder. His staff became a sword. This would not take long. He would have plenty of time to change back before the meeting with Qurong and Marak.

One last look in the mirror. His own mother wouldn't recognize him—much less Cassak.

TWO

The march back into Middle was quiet. No fanfare, no fuss—the way Cassak preferred it. He barked at the gatekeeper, who let him through, then took his prisoners down the main road, past vendors and merchants, toward the officers' hall where Marak had barricaded himself. The lake came up on their left, and the palace was ahead on the right.

He mopped sweat, morst, and grime from his forehead and silently maligned the priest, his Throaters, the rebels, and finally Marak for the indecision that had forced his hand, for being so bullheaded with all of this.

The entire mess was simple, but Sucrow, Marak, Qurong, and Eram seemed bent on complicating things. Hang them all. It was only midmorning, and he'd already ridden all over Middle and a good portion of desert.

"Captain, a word," Josef said.

"What is it, runt?"

Josef kept his eyes up the road. The young man was strange, his skin shimmery white against his black horse, and his gray-white eyes tinted with that strange purple hue. "I know how those three albinos got in and out of the attic in the palace. Interested?"

Cassak frowned. "How is that?"

"That's for me to know." Josef gave a wicked grin. Now his eyes almost glowed. His skin was nigh translucent. Unnerving. "You've heard of albino magic, haven't you?"

Cassak considered this. He wasn't sure what he thought about the albino sorcery, but this nobody had the attentions of the general, the priest, and now Qurong himself. He waited.

"They have books in which they've written their spells and incantations," Josef continued. "It's where things such as the amulet come from."

Curious. Marak might find the information useful.

Cassak's eyes narrowed. "And?"

"I have one of their books," Josef explained. He withdrew a leather book bound with red twine from beneath his tunic and showed him the worn, bloodstained cover. "They were after the rest of them, left inside the palace. Without them they cannot complete a ritual that they must—within the next week."

"How do you know these things?"

"I was slave to them for a time. Did you search the attic?"

"Of course."

"Search it again. Look everywhere, inside everything. Bring them to me. Then you will see."

Of course he would. Marak would be irritated if the priest found them first. In fact, the priest was likely the reason the books were missing. But he didn't want this youth knowing his interest.

Cassak pushed away from Josef. "I have things to do."

"Just go look, Captain."

The captain mulled it over. Finally, "If you're lying, I'm telling Marak to slit your throat."

"That won't be necessary."

"We will see."

Cassak rode ahead. Idly he scratched at a spot on his arm. The sunlight grew hazy and strange, making it difficult to see. He shielded his eyes and pressed on. Soon footsteps drew his attention. He squinted to see, one hand on his sword.

A young scout approached and dropped to his knee. Cassak stopped his horse and nodded. Relaxed.

Something sweet wafted in the air. For some reason Cassak felt disembodied, dizzy. He shook off the numbing sensation. His eyes fixed on those of the scout. Curious, this was.

His eyes narrowed. The scout rose, offering a small blue star. Cassak inspected it. "What is this?"

"A gift," the scout replied. "From my son."

Cassak continued to stare at the little star. His skin prickled. He should send the scout away, tell him to take his silly trinket and leave. But as he watched, the star shifted, turning into the eye of a serpent before melting into his palm and becoming part of his skin. Then it disappeared.

He rubbed his palm, unnerved and riveted by the sight.

"What does it do?" Cassak's own voice sounded distant, constricted. He looked again at his palm. Cold to the touch.

The scout's lip curled into a strange smile. Cassak found it difficult to breathe and more difficult to break eye contact with this scout, whom he suddenly realized he didn't recognize.

"Allows your eyes to see."

Cassak shook his head, trying to clear it.

When he looked up, the scout was gone.

What in the world just happened?

They were coming up on the officers' hall, surrounded by fifty men, windows sealed with iron bars. No one could see in or even get close enough to try. Cassak caught himself staring at his hand.

Josef was watching him.

"What?" Cassak barked.

"Just wondering who that was."

"A scout."

"Well, yes, but could it have—"

"I've had enough of your mouth." They approached the guard. "In."

CASSAK'S WARRIORS PRODDED JOHNIS AND SILVIE THROUGH the halls and into a dark war room where Marak stood waiting.

The haze intensified. A salty, copper taste flooded Johnis's mouth. He needed to further the mission. Further their revenge.

With the end of the Circle came the end of the Horde.

With the conquer of the Horde came the end of Teeleh. The end of Teeleh and the beginning of something new.

"Kneel." A rough hand shoved Johnis to his knees. Silvie thumped to the ground next to him. Cassak brushed past him and gave Marak the amulet.

The general turned it over in his hand. Studied the small thing that had caused so much trouble. Looked perturbed.

"You two have caused me a lot of grief," he said.

"It's not my fault the rebels attacked."

"It's your fault the priest went on this cursed fool's hunt."

Johnis bristled. Shaeda didn't like this. Neither did he.

With Shaeda's heightened senses, he became aware of everything: The long, oval table surrounded by chairs. Pillar candles casting eerie shadows. Torches on six-foot stands, unlit. The place made him think of a Shataiki lair, made him edgy. Or was that Shaeda?

He could set the place ablaze, storm into the thrall, and demand Sucrow comply. He could end this now. He could . . .

His eyes fixed on the amulet. Shaeda's focus soaked into his flesh, rushing over his body like a waterfall, a broken dam spilling into the ocean and sweeping him away in the riptide.

Marak held the medallion. *He hinders the mission.*

No. Offer a truce first. Waste not, want not. Shaeda couldn't argue with that.

Johnis looked Marak straight in the eye. The man found honesty impressive. So Johnis would give him impressive. They had no time to waste with all this.

"I'm the reason they were there, then. Drawing attention to your men."

"Josef," Silvie whispered.

His mind shifted. Silvie was the key to subverting Shaeda, to harnessing the Leedhan's power on his own. And he was almost positive he knew how.

Marak studied him. He dragged a chair with his foot and shoved it in front of Johnis. "Sit. Your girl can take the other."

There were only two chairs.

Johnis scowled. He helped Silvie stand, then let her have the chair. A second one was dragged from the table, and only then did he sit.

"Why is Sucrow interested in this medallion?"

Johnis laughed. A husky laugh that came from Shaeda. "General, that amulet is the key to your trouble. Think of it."

Marak eyed him. For a moment his eyes went to his captain. Then back to Johnis. He didn't look convinced. "This amulet."

Shaeda took over. Johnis could feel her magic course through him. Her eyes, it was all about her eyes . . .

"Yes. That amulet. Come on, Marak. Surely a general knows appearances are deceptive."

Marak's expression became unreadable. What was she doing to the general?

"Press the matter."

"Release us. Make alliance with myself and Arya. Once the priest has outworn his uses, we'll be rid of him."

Marak's gray eyes searched both of them. "And why should I be interested in an alliance?"

"Because you can do it my way, in the time frame Qurong wants," he said. Shaeda said. Was there a difference anymore?

Silvie touched his arm. Shaeda bristled.

"You already made your bed," Marak reminded.

"Warryn and his men were uninvited guests. Sucrow turned me down, and I came alone. The Throaters decided to tag along anyway."

"I'm not interested. You change loyalties too quickly."

For some reason that stung. He shoved it aside. "Come now, General, we both know that isn't true. You don't like the priest, and you won't let him have the credit for getting rid of the albinos, either."

Marak fell quiet.

Alliance or death. *"Which will it be, General?"*

Shaeda chuckled in Johnis's head. Her power of influence had no limitation, save that of a human conductor.

"You have a plan, then."

"I always have a plan, General." He and Silvie had discussed this, and Shaeda's foresight had let him see all the way to a place called Ba'al Bek, from whence they would unleash the Shataiki on the albinos.

Marak's eyes narrowed. "I don't require you to use it."

"You assume you have all the pieces. Would I have asked for the priest's help if I didn't have to?" The general seemed not to remember the harach fruit. Johnis didn't intend to remind him of it until he'd secured him as an ally.

Marak still didn't seem quite convinced. He hadn't forgotten that Johnis had gone to the priest first. He stood. "Cassak, keep these two under guard."

Johnis jumped up. "General, if you keep us in custody, we remain a liability. If you release us, we can help you defend this place against the Throaters."

Marak glared at him. Shaeda was working, but he was so stubborn.

"Do you want the amulet that close to Sucrow?" Johnis watched. Could Marak be manipulated? "I can't help you if I'm tied up. And Sucrow is likely to intercept that medallion the second you walk out of there."

Marak still didn't look ready to play ball. A muscle in his jaw twitched. "When I return."

"Trust begins somewhere, General. And neither of us has any sentiments toward the priest. He took your family, I heard."

Marak's fist curled into a hard knot.

"We could do something about that, you and I." It was out before Johnis really had time to think about it, but now he was glad Shaeda's foresight had come through.

The general passed the amulet to Cassak. The shackles fell

from Johnis's wrists. He resisted the impulse to rub them. Bit back a pleased smile. So Shaeda had uses beyond physical strength as well. Surely he already knew that.

"Don't lose sight of the amulet, General."

Shaeda's vision overpowered Johnis, turning his focus toward the desert, toward Ba'al Bek. He required blood and sacrifice . . . Blood so full of iron he could taste the metal in his mouth. The Circle and the Horde would die by this plague, and a new era would begin. One of power and might. One where all bowed to—

"Josef," Silvie interrupted.

He blinked. Marak was waiting for an answer to a question Johnis hadn't heard. Shaeda was in a hurry; she was always in a hurry. The slower her movements appeared, the more haste she required.

"We don't have time to waste. The window of opportunity grows short. The amulet's guardian will come for his trophy."

"Guardian," Marak repeated.

"I highly doubt you wish to be the one holding that amulet when the queen, Derias, comes for it."

The general's eyes narrowed, as if considering whether or not that was a threat. He turned to leave. "Don't do anything foolish."

DARSAL WAS ALONE IN THE GENERAL'S CHAMBER. SHE HAD eavesdropped a few minutes before hearing more than she cared to, and now wished to consider her options in private. She studied the room. A bedroll. A table. Two journals, side by side—one Martyn's war journal, one Rona's. They were the two sides of her Scab general. One cunning and tactical, stoic and cold. One warm and full of barely restrained passion.

She fingered Jordan's necklace.

Everything began to sink in. So much to reclaim. So much lost. Romania and the Black Forest and old Middle Forest haunted her, whispering specters in the back of her mind.

"Where are our vows now?" she grumbled, her eyes narrowed. The shock of hearing Johnis talk like that had worn off, and now the summer's heat of anger stirred up inside her.

Follow your heart, Thomas, then Johnis, had always said.

"My heart wants to beat some sense into him."

Frustrated, she groaned. Part of her remembered she was a slave and would be summoned at any moment. But for now she was free to rage.

A gentle laugh tittered through the room. Darsal whirled, landed in a crouch. Marak had extra knives in a small trunk. How to get to them?

Her eyes widened.

A furry white bat with round, green eyes was laughing at her. It took her a second to realize who and what it was.

Darsal's arms fell to her sides. "Gabil?"

"Well, yes, I believe that is my name. I trust you haven't forgotten me."

"Forgotten—Where have you *been*?" she snapped at him.

"That isn't important, and it isn't why I'm here." He hopped toward her, wings slapping the air.

"Do you know the half of what's been going on over here? Johnis and Silvie, and—"

"Oh, yes." Gabil turned serious for half a second. "Yes, I'm afraid it's been a dreadful time."

"You didn't bother warning us. Didn't bother to tell us we all had to drown!"

Gabil waited until she was looking at him again. "No, I suppose we didn't."

"Johnis and Silvie are rotten through because no one told us we had to—" She stopped.

"Well, Darsal, you knew you had to find water, didn't you?"

"But not to drown. No one would just decide to do that."

"You did, didn't you?"

She scoffed. "I had Jordan."

"So why do you assume it's all a loss?"

She didn't answer.

"What did Elyon tell you, Darsal?"

"'Return to the Horde, and love them for me. For Johnis.'"

"Yes, for Johnis. Ultimately, though, Darsal, it isn't about you. It's about Elyon. This saving the Circle—most of whom you've never met—learning to love a Scab . . ."

"Elyon." She let the name spread over her tongue and fill her mouth. Her fury subsided. Whatever happened, Elyon was here, and Gabil was in front of her, destined to drive her crazy.

She dropped down and hugged her old friend. Ran her fingers through his fur.

Gabil laughed. "That's a much better welcome, if I do say so myself. And that tickles."

Darsal sat down. Pulled one knee up and propped her chin on it. "Well, it's been awful. Where's Thomas, the Forest Guard—I mean, Circle? Why is the Horde in Middle?" The flood of questions continued. She couldn't help it, now that someone with answers was right in front of her. "We lost the books, Gabil. We had to leave them in the attic. I don't know how we'll get them back. All that trouble for nothing."

The Roush shook his head. "Maybe the books weren't meant for you, child. Did you consider that?"

No, she hadn't.

Darsal let that thought sink in. Then, "So what do I do? Why here, now? How does loving the Horde—Marak—save the Circle?"

"That is a mystery. I suppose you keep doing what you've been doing."

"Fight with Marak, and pray Johnis and Silvie come to their senses? Yes, that's helping so much." She started thinking out loud. "They're Horde. They've turned their backs on everything, Gabil. Everything. Johnis went to the priest. To Sucrow. I swear, he's possessed."

Gabil became very, very quiet. Unnervingly so. "So he is."

"What's wrong with him? His eyes and skin are all wrong. And please don't tell me it's the scabbing disease. It's beyond that."

A long pause.

"Gabil, please."

"Patience. I'm trying to decide what I can tell you. Yes, in a sense Johnis is possessed, by a Leedhan. She calls herself an entity . . ." His expression was unreadable. "Half-Shataiki, half-Horde."

Darsal furrowed her brow.

"Her name is Shaeda."

"The Leedhan."

He nodded. "She wishes to conquer the Horde and the Circle as part of a plot to exact revenge on Teeleh. A spiteful, evil creature."

Darsal's eyes narrowed. "That won't happen."

The Roush tensed. Hesitated. "I would focus on what you can do, not what you can't, Darsal."

"You aren't helping, Gabil."

"Well, keep talking. We'll come up with something, I'm sure of it. Certainly a plan will take form. I have all confidence."

She was back to wanting to smack the oversized white bat.

"Well, go on," he urged.

Darsal took a long, deep breath. "If I help Johnis and Marak, the Circle dies. If I take out the priest, it'll fall on Johnis, Marak, or both."

"Or you."

"I'm beside the point!" she snapped. "If my death serves the mission, so be it."

"Now you sound like Johnis."

Darsal ground her teeth. "I need an immediate solution."

Even as she said it, she knew what she would do. She was Elyon's emissary, sent to bring him the hearts of Scabs. Marak was one. Now there were two more.

"I need to see Johnis."

Gabil eyed her but offered no indication on her course of action. "Well, whatever you decide, hurry, as I believe your general is returning. And he's in a foul mood, I might add."

Darsal fingered her pendant, eyes narrow. "We'll see."

THREE

Sucrow retreated to his chambers and completed the ritual to undo his facade of the young scout. Then he started for the palace to meet Marak and Qurong. As he neared the palace, he spotted Cassak up the road, taking orders from Marak. He sneered, pleased at the obvious rift in their friendship. The captain turned to summon the commanders. Anxious. And foolish to think that he could keep Teeleh's priest out of the officers' hall with a simple barricade.

How easily the loyal dog of the general was enticed.

Sucrow cackled. "Ambitious little captain, is he not?" He watched Cassak until the captain broke away from the others. Warryn was in place for his next assignment.

Now for the next item of business. What was that old saying? "That which bends not, break shall." Marak would bow before Lord Teeleh—one way or another.

"Let us see what can be done for the captain's ambition," Sucrow muttered to himself. "Surely he has better thoughts of glory than his brazen general."

Cassak broke off from the commanders outside Marak's quarters and started back up the street as the others went inside.

Sucrow followed, slowly catching up. At last he was abreast of the man. Cassak glanced over, a scowl on his face.

"What do you want?" the captain snapped.

So angry, this one was. Pleased, Sucrow withdrew a sidna and took a bite. He twisted his staff. A strange light seeped out—noticeable only to those with eyes to see.

"Warryn maintains you provoked the Eramites," Sucrow said, still looking ahead. He chewed slowly and swallowed, watched Cassak tense as the spell took root. Oh, yes, already the little charm was doing its work, crawling beneath the skin into the captain's heart. "But we both know my chieftain has a tendency to exaggerate, don't we?"

Cassak's scowl hardened. His eyes briefly landed on his own palm. Most excellent. Sucrow could barely contain the excitement, the thrill of the hunt, the rush of adrenaline involved whenever his spell fell over a new victim.

"Of course, I will have to inform Qurong." Sucrow raised a brow. "What say you?"

The captain remained edgy. Tendrils of shadow swirled around his throat and constricted. The others never seemed to notice. Curious. Blind, all of them.

"What's your game, Priest?"

"It is not for holy men to engage in petty games, Captain. Rather, we strive to bring instruction and exhortation, to train the sons of men." Mentally Sucrow recited an incantation, a mantra opening the captain's mind further to suggestion. Treacherous thoughts that could drive a wedge between Marak and Cassak. A wedge not even an albino wench could remove.

Marak of Southern wasn't really all he seemed, was he? Loyalty, integrity, and honor, he'd taught. And yet his loyalty betrayed his family to his supreme commander, then his supreme commander—and his own people—to an albino. What did that say of loyalty, of integrity? And what did his arrogance say of honor?

Self-imposed honor, perhaps. Naught else.

Cassak's gaze fell again to his hand. Of course, by now the little star had migrated to his throat, the jugular. "And what might your teaching to a warrior be, Priest?"

Sucrow retrieved a fruit from his robes. "Would you care for a sidna, Captain? They are quite delicious." A simple fruit, nothing more. The true magic was in what he had already done. The fruit was merely a personal joke, a private symbolism. Marak would have understood it, oddly.

Cassak, however, did not. Dumb ox.

"A sidna?"

"It is from the north forest." He extended the fruit in his hand. For a second the captain looked offended at the offer, then seemed to think better of his own offense. He accepted the sidna.

Sucrow watched Cassak bite, turning his staff in his hand, keeping the end level with Cassak. The captain's eyes changed, and he tugged the collar of his tunic. "Is your general displeased with you?"

"I grow weary of your questions, Priest. Don't you have a reckoning with Qurong?"

Bitter fool, wasn't he? How terribly disappointing to catch a smaller fish because the larger one refuses to be caught. But still, the smaller could be set to catch the larger.

Cassak's pupils shrank to needle points. His eyes took on the same greenish-yellow cast as Sucrow's other serpent warriors, a cast they themselves could not see. Yes, this captain would become a great general, one who heeded the servants of Teeleh rather than his own foolhardy ambitions.

There we are, my fool.

"I was merely curious," Sucrow said. "You manage to prevent a war, and yet the general finds no cause to promote you? Many less experienced have already surpassed you."

Cassak's face hardened. Ah, the great captain's underbelly. He'd done so much for Marak, only to be left behind while Marak climbed the ranks.

"That is not your concern. It is you who almost caused it."

Incompetent serpent warrior, Sucrow thought. "All of Middle is my concern. We all serve the Great One, no?"

More hesitation. Sucrow knew most of Marak's men didn't

directly serve Teeleh, but all feared him, even more than their general.

"Think on it, Captain. I must be gone now. I have a high position available, one more suited to you, and I have favor with Qurong. Come and see me should you reconsider."

THIN LIGHT STREAMED FROM A CRACKLING TORCH. THEY were in an office converted into a bedroom. No windows, only a single torch stand. Two cots and a trunk made up the whole of the furnishings.

"Ba'al Bek," Johnis said to Silvie. She leaned against the wall, arms folded. Marak had ordered a servant to give them clean clothes and allow them weapons. A show of good faith, so it seemed.

And now Shaeda disclosed the next stage. Her patience was running thin. Her thoughts opened, and he saw barren desert and the high place she called Ba'al Bek and a throng of Shataiki led by Derias . . .

"We need to go to Ba'al Bek."

"Why?" Silvie shifted forward. "That takes longer, Johnis." She lifted a brow. "We need a plan, love. We aren't pretending to do her will if we never work to undermine her."

He hesitated.

"Is she listening?" Silvie asked.

"I . . . can't tell. She's not strangling me right now."

"What's your heart say?"

Johnis swallowed. "She's likely always in my head, and occasionally allows me enough rope to hang myself if she so chooses. She's manipulative."

Silvie scoffed, but didn't comment. They couldn't plan an escape if Shaeda was always listening. He had but two advantages: Silvie alone could command his attentions over Shaeda's. And Shaeda's wishes were always open to interpretation.

"But you can't stop trying. And she can't possibly be everywhere at once."

"I don't think she has to be, anymore than I do." His focus shifted. "We're going to Ba'al Bek because it's one of Teeleh's holy places, which is why Shaeda feels compelled to desecrate it. She hates him, Silvie. Despises him. You've never felt anything like it." Johnis paused. "We just have to assume her power before . . ."

Shaeda cinched her grip on him. Silvie's eyes narrowed. For a long minute the Leedhan glowered at Silvie through Johnis, and Silvie returned the glare.

"Johnis. Silvie."

Johnis's hand went for the sword that one of Marak's men had given him. He and Silvie exchanged glances—no one here knew them by those names. An albino entered—Marak's slave. She wore a scarf over her head and face. Clanking metal. A length of chain ran between her ankles. Dark eyes searched their faces.

Darsal.

Darsal was an albino. An enemy. She would try to stop Shaeda's plans. Johnis's plans.

No, that wasn't true. Darsal wasn't the enemy.

The talons clawed at him. Yes, yes, she will do all to thwart them, should she know . . .

Silvie scowled, hands falling to her knives. "What do you want?"

Darsal pushed back her hood, revealing smooth skin painted white with morst. Long, dark hair, braided in Horde fashion.

"To see you," she said. Her gaze swept over Silvie, then Johnis. "What . . . happened?"

"You little leech." Silvie looked like a viper. "You left us for the Horde."

Darsal caught her breath. "I was captured, Silvie," she said simply. She was working hard not to stare at Johnis. "What is going on?"

Johnis scowled. His lip curled into a snarl. Shaeda saw albino meat—an enemy that must die.

Darsal took a step back. "I heard you have a Leedhan. An entity. Very self-indulgent term, if you ask me."

"And why would you care?" Silvie demanded.

Darsal stared Johnis in the face. All he could see was her smooth albino skin covered in white paste, and her rich, dark eyes enhanced by a single scar. She would bleed red.

Johnis didn't want Darsal dead. Not now. But she hindered the mission.

"I saw Gabil," Darsal said. "And Elyon."

Shaeda hissed. Johnis hissed. "You're lying."

"I swear on the books," Darsal said.

The books. He wondered if Cassak had located the others yet. Odd that Darsal would make such a vow now.

Johnis scowled. "You betrayed us."

"Johnis . . . trust me."

He recoiled. "Why would we listen to a treacherous Shataiki-lover like you?"

"Because you *forgave* me! Don't you remember, Johnis? You saved me."

Footsteps echoed in the hall, cutting her short. She glanced over her shoulder. "Remember, Johnis. Elyon—it's all about Elyon."

He bristled at the name.

Angry shouts and a skirmish in the hall echoed through the door. They all jumped. Johnis and Silvie drew their blades. Darsal hid behind the door.

The knob turned. Men with tan robes and drawn, crimson-stained swords poured into the room, aiming straight for Johnis. He heard Darsal drop one, unconscious, behind him. Silvie's knife pinned the next assailant to the wall. A second flashed out. Johnis swung his own blade. Metal grated against metal.

His attacker sliced into his shoulder. Johnis blocked the next blow and slashed a diagonal arc with enough force to sever the man's torso.

Another was on him. Johnis almost lost his balance but used the momentum to spin sideways and catch the man between the ribs.

Darsal had found someone's knife and drew an opponent out into the hall. Johnis heard a yelp and a crash and nothing more.

A blow from behind knocked him flat. He rolled. The assailant struck him in the head. He saw a flashing light and tried not to pass out. Thrust with his sword. It clattered across the hard floor. Johnis kicked.

His arms were pinned. A knee drove between his shoulder blades. Johnis wrestled loose. *Shaeda!* He tried to invoke her power.

Silvie shouted. Someone struck her, and she fell. Silence. Hellish silence. Where had the Leedhan gone . . . ?

Johnis swept his attacker's feet from under him and slashed down with his sword. An intruder dove into the hall with an unconscious Silvie over his shoulder. More shouting.

What should he do?

The priest. It had to be the priest. Johnis grabbed an iron poker and rammed it between the bars on the window and the wood surrounding. He ripped away the barrier and jumped through the window. Ran around the side of the building and darted down an alleyway. They wouldn't risk taking Silvie down the main road. He wouldn't bother trying to catch up and overpower that many men.

Instead he raced for the temple.

Shaeda had not given him her strength. As they ran closer, her thoughts grew erratic, senses heightened. She was . . . nervous? Invisible talons drove into him. Raked over his body. Johnis bit his lip so he wouldn't cry out.

Just as before, his loyalty, his love for Silvie, overpowered Shaeda's stranglehold. Her grip slipped. He pressed on.

Johnis caught up to the Throaters and raced up the temple steps to meet them at the top. He drew his sword, but suddenly Shaeda overwhelmed him, forced his knees to buckle.

No! They have Silvie! I must save her from the priest!

Shaeda growled in his head. The Throaters came at him. Johnis struggled, but the Leedhan was too strong. Everything grew hazy and purple, then faded . . .

FOUR

"My general and my priest," Qurong mocked. "What's a ruler to do when he grants his priest authority over his general, only to have the priest prove less competent than the general?" The supreme commander had spent the better part of an hour upbraiding both Marak and Sucrow, and Marak was more than ready to move on.

"My lord—" Marak began, even though at the moment Qurong was raging against Sucrow.

His leader continued his rant. "No! You saw an opportunity to show off, and you failed miserably, Priest! Now, give me one reason I shouldn't just execute the both of you and start over with this newcomer who claims he can do both your jobs!"

"Respectfully, my lord, he cannot," Marak interjected.

Qurong swerved and demanded a report. Marak told him

everything—beginning with the arrival of the mysterious couple, Josef and Arya, and ending with his reasons for refusing to turn over the amulet and the prisoners.

"A Leedhan." Qurong bristled.

"Yes, my lord," Sucrow answered. "The boy's account fits the legends."

The supreme commander glared at Marak. "Where is the amulet the priest wished in his possession?"

Tread lightly, Jordan would have told him. *Don't be hasty, brother. Don't accept power when you don't trust the source.*

"It is in safe keeping, my lord, secured along with the two prisoners."

"And so you've defied my orders to report to the priest?" Qurong demanded. "Have you gone the way of the rebels?"

"No, my lord. I have not. And I—"

"And the wench Sucrow wanted is now dead?"

Marak tensed.

This pleased the priest. Sucrow was smirking at him, staff in hand. Marak felt light-headed and angry. Jordan's chiding voice echoed in his mind.

Marak cleared his throat. "My lord," he spoke in a very low voice. "Those albinos were executed days ago."

"You finally proved man enough to do it, then," Qurong sneered. He glanced at the slave near his general, saw the little pendant she was wearing, and scowled.

Jordan would tell him not to go through with this.

Don't accept evil to further good, he would say.

Why not?

Marak, you bullheaded idiot. What good comes of wiping out an entire race of people?

Marak was barely listening to Qurong and Sucrow, even as Sucrow went on about the Leedhan's capabilities. He should be paying attention, but he couldn't with this strange feeling nagging at him.

He threw the priest a glare. Sucrow seemed uninterested. No, he was . . . manipulating them?

"My lord," Marak interrupted, "If this expedition mounts and proves successful, all of the albinos, including Thomas of Hunter, will be dead in a matter of days. And I prefer to conduct my own interrogations since the priest's serpent warriors seem to have a fascination with cutting out prisoners' tongues before they've a chance to talk."

Qurong threw the priest a dirty look. "Is that so?"

"A rare occurrence, my lord," the priest assured, his staff turning in his hand. "It's the mongrel he last gave me he's so irritable about. But she was worth nothing."

Marak's attention snapped back. His hand curled around his hilt.

"Now, on to this albino and Shataiki business," Qurong growled. "Speak, General. Don't allow a priest to outdo you."

Marak remained unwilling to give his superior the satisfaction of a reaction.

"Oh," Qurong taunted. "The general doesn't like my assessment." He chuckled. "Of course, if that whelp succeeds, he'll have made fools of you both. You are supposed to be my best. Frankly, I'm disappointed."

"He found a harach, my lord," Sucrow interjected. "He has no idea what to do with it on his own."

"So you are holding out on me," Marak growled.

"Maybe you aren't as perceptive as you used to be, General," Sucrow sneered. "Your vision seems blurry these days. Losing your edge, perhaps? Your captain certainly thinks so."

Cassak.

Marak knew better, though. Or did he? What was Sucrow up to? His eyes narrowed. He forced a direct gaze, sizing up the man with the staff. Sucrow had never, to his knowledge, performed any sorcery on him.

But this strange sense of unease . . . Was Sucrow threatening or taunting him?

Finally Marak answered, choosing to pretend nothing was suspicious. "Keep it up, Priest."

He could have sworn Sucrow blinked.

Unaccustomed to being suspected so early, aren't you, Priest?

The priest broke eye contact. The constricted, numbing sensation left. "You wouldn't dare."

"Try me." Marak's hand remained on his sword.

"Stand down, General," Qurong warned. "Priest, speak."

A dark look crossed the priest's face. What was he plotting

now? Would Sucrow have Cassak killed just to demoralize Marak?

Cold fingers slid up his back. It would work, too.

"I fail to see where the medallion comes in." Qurong glared. "Get to the point."

"The point, my lord," Sucrow replied, "is that while little is known of these things, the legends themselves exist."

Marak narrowed his eyes. He had no desire to run all over the desert chasing a legend. But he'd given Josef and Arya his word. And they were convinced they could finish off the Circle in three days. Sucrow wanted in, and that was all the convincing Marak needed.

He would do whatever it took to get Qurong off his back and put the priest in his place. Most curious was that not even Qurong had heard of the Leedhan.

Qurong spoke, his eyes wide with conspiracy, as if some ancient favor had come to him from the sky. "So there really is an amulet that controls these . . . things."

Sucrow handed Qurong his book. "The kind of tree that produced the wood it's made from supposedly no longer exists. He showed us the harach earlier, and I thought, perhaps if it does exist, we can be rid of the vermin more quickly." The priest sneered. "Be rid of our general's hesitation."

Marak white-knuckled his belt, fighting the urge to bash in the priest's head. "Why involve a human?" he asked.

Sucrow laughed hard and loud. "We are catalysts. We live in two worlds, Marak. Haven't you realized that?"

Marak didn't comment.

"An expedition may well be worthwhile, to rid ourselves of them once and for all. It is quite simple. We gain control of this Shataiki amulet guardian, invoke a ceremony on Ba'al Bek, and unleash the Shataiki on the albinos."

Qurong was so lost in thought he didn't seem to hear them anymore. He turned to go. "I will do this: you will both go, with equal authority and equal standing. You will mount this expedition, and—provided you don't kill each other—both return with the Shataiki on a leash and a solution for your stupidity with the rebels. If either of those directives fail, I will hold you both responsible. You have two days. Am I clear?"

"My lord—" Sucrow started.

"Begone."

MARAK HAD BARELY LEFT THE PALACE BEFORE CASSAK CAME galloping back up the road for him, Marak's mount in tow. He swung up, knife in hand. His face was flushed, eyes wide, pupils tiny.

"There's been a breach, General," Cassak announced. "The whole building's coming—"

"Who is it?" Marak snapped, suddenly frustrated. Sucrow snickered from behind. A chill swept over him. Marak checked his pocket for the amulet as he raced back with Cassak.

"Don't know yet, sir. No insignias. We're assuming Eram."

Eram. Cassak had no business making assumptions.

Marak grumbled. "Who's on the roof?"

"Six archers. My men are gone; Reyan's are divided. We don't know how they breached the blockade."

Bloody Eram. He never should have trusted that half-breed Horde trickster and his bunch of ex–Forest Guard in the first place.

He and Cassak reached the hall, where men were beating each other down with swords.

"They're ransacking everything," a fighter said.

"Take a hostage," Marak growled. He swung off his horse and rushed into the hall. Ran an invader through and rolled him over. Cassak was right—no identifying insignia. But why would Eram go through the trouble to mask his men's identity?

Unless it wasn't Eram after all . . .

The general whipped around and let fly one of his knives into someone's temple. He cut down a third.

Someone was going to pay for this.

FIVE

Striking the cold, hard floor, Johnis woke. He heard Silvie yelp and tried to sit up.

"Let me go!" she demanded.

Shaeda was quiet, too quiet. Everything was foggy, dreamlike. Another kind of darkness lingered here.

The Throaters dragged Johnis to his knees and pushed him forward onto his palms. The bag was ripped from his head, yanking strands of hair with it.

Johnis squinted in the dim candlelight. He'd needed the images that Shaeda's gift of foresight could offer. Why had she allowed the Throaters to take him? But that was it, wasn't it? To prove he needed her, not the other way around. He had to find a way to keep her power but get her claws out of him.

"Bloody priest," Silvie spat. She was on his left. Her face was tense, lips pressed together, eyes narrowed. A deep, fresh gash oozed blood just over her brow. A red trickle made its way down the side of her pallid cheek and off her jaw to her shoulder and the ground.

Her knuckles were raw. Her limbs pulled as tightly against her restraints as she could manage. Even on all fours, her snakelike eyes had fixed on someone in front of her and refused to be distracted.

The door locked behind them. Johnis raised his head to see the object of Silvie's killing gaze: a skinny, black-hooded Scab with white skin flaking to the point of disfigurement, dripping in gaudy jewelry. His hawkish expression leered at them.

Sucrow.

This time he did not need Shaeda's influence. Nor did he want it.

Johnis rose to his knees and rolled his shoulders back. His muscles tightened. The invisible claws tore at his back, but he fought through the pain. Shaeda's talons and Sucrow's magic pulled him in opposite directions.

A small metallic sound rang from behind and to the left of Johnis. An apprentice had a silver knife at Silvie's throat. The only change in her expression was that she looked much angrier.

Sucrow wanted to play with them. Pungent incense wafted from a bowl on the far side of the room, next to what looked like another shrine and hundreds of feathered serpents that represented Teeleh. Just off center was Sucrow's altar, much like the one they recently encountered in the Black Forest. Narrow grooves were carved out of the rim to catch blood and guide it into a small silver tray below.

Johnis tried not to shudder as Shaeda's fear and hatred of the Shataiki overtook him. A purple-and-blue haze fell on him. He could feel every ounce of her disgust at the winged-serpent image. At the Dark Priest.

"What do you want, Priest?"

"Respect," the priest said. "Your loyalty."

Johnis growled. "I give respect where it is due, Priest."

A fist struck him from behind. Johnis buckled under the blow and saw yellow and blue flashes of light. He righted himself and shook it off.

Shaeda's thoughts turned dark, knocking the wind out of him. She was strangling him. *Shaeda*, he managed. *You're killing me . . .*

She loosed her grip a little, still tense. Her talons still cut into him, so great was her hatred of all things Teeleh.

Release me! he protested.

The talons dug harder, pinching him. "*Put aside these thoughts of freedom. Freedom for you shall come with death.*"

Sucrow laughed. "Still struggling with glorious delusions, Chosen One?"

"I don't know what you mean."

"Does Sucrow know? How?"

The priest forced Johnis's head sideways and traced his crescent-shaped birthmark—the one behind his ear—with his fingernails. Chuckled.

"Oh yes, Witch spoke of you, before Ciphus killed him," Sucrow taunted. "And then I killed Ciphus. And now, you, Chosen One."

Sorcerors, to the last of them. Johnis's skin crawled under the touch. He fought the impulse to recoil out of sheer revulsion. In the end pride quelled his horror.

"Drop dead," Silvie snapped.

"Arya," Johnis scolded, refusing to confirm what Sucrow already gathered.

"Pity that wench who bore you had to die."

Johnis ground his teeth. Sucrow chuckled, still stroking along Johnis's neck, sending the tingling down his arms and legs. He scrutinized his prey. Reached for the ring on Johnis's hand. His mother's ring.

Johnis curled his hand into a fist. The Dark Priest sneered. He pressed into Johnis's skin, digging at his flesh until he made a ragged cut. Johnis winced.

"You've caused me enough trouble." Sucrow grabbed Johnis by the hair and jerked his head up. "I want to make something perfectly clear so that you understand your place. Agreeable, don't you think?"

A Throater shoved Silvie to her feet, knife still at her throat, and forced her to the edge of the altar. Her movements were stiff, as if under some spell. She was made to climb on top and lie down on her back.

He chained her to the wood.

Silvie craned her neck and shot Johnis a desperate look. "Jo . . . sef . . ."

She had almost used his real name.

Blood pounded in his temple; his hate rose. He channeled both into a rage and lunged against his shackles. Surely Shaeda would give him strength. Strength to tear off these shackles and destroy the priest who dared touch Silvie.

"She stays with me!"

Nothing. He was helpless.

Shaeda.

Sucrow cackled. "You understand, then. Insurance."

MARAK WAS COVERED IN BLOOD. HE FOUGHT HIS WAY DOWN the hall toward Josef and Arya's room in time to see Darsal knife-fighting with an enemy. She sliced into his upper arm and ducked low to keep from tripping. Why didn't she kill the man?

"Darsal!"

Another intruder. Marak fought him off, took a graze to the ear. He heard a crash and Darsal's yelp cut short. Marak whirled and saw her motionless on the floor.

His heart lurched.

Marak was on the man before he knew what he was doing. Her opponent slammed into the wall. Marak's sword fell toward him. Their blades clanged together. Marak blocked a blow. Feinted and sliced a diagonal arc.

The intruder blocked with such force it rattled Marak's arms. Marak dodged another and slashed against the man's abdomen, disarmed him, then slashed off his head.

Marak burst into the room that served Josef and Arya and spun around in time to block an attack. He pivoted sideways, unwilling to be trapped by a wall.

A hard hit slammed him to his knees. Blood oozed from his shoulder. Marak blocked again. The sword rose up. Fell.

Then his attacker fell. Marak rammed his knife into the man's throat.

Darsal kicked the dead man aside and wiped her stolen sword on his tunic. "My general."

She extended her hand. He jumped up and knocked the blade from her hand. Instantly Darsal punched him in the chest, then went into a defensive stance.

"Darsal," he growled. She was alive. He could kiss her. Slap her.

Settle down, idiot. She's alive. Thank Teeleh, she's alive.

She straightened. "You're welcome," she snapped.

Cassak came into the room with several warriors. He tried not to gawk at the albino with blood all over her. What was he staring at, anyway? He'd seen a female albino before. Especially this one.

"They're gone," she said.

Thank Teeleh he still had the medallion. Yes, Cassak had barely stopped a war with the Eramites. But his messages had been growing increasingly inappropriate. His interference had cost Marak his entire family, and Qurong's trust.

Sucrow's mockery echoed in his head.

The surge of frustration continued, though Marak wasn't entirely sure why he was so angry with his captain, his lifelong friend.

Of course, Cassak had stood there and watched the priest torture Jordan and Rona. Cassak had carried out Marak's order to kill them while Marak watched. Cassak had suggested the use of the Desecration on them. Cassak wanted Darsal to die just as badly as the priest.

Cassak had been in command of this stronghold. Only he had access. Only he could have caused the breach.

Sucrow was right about one thing.

"General, they're—"

Marak exploded.

"Did the entire watch fall asleep at the same time?" he screamed in Cassak's face. "Was the only person awake in the whole building an albino slave?"

"We're looking into—"

"Get the scouts on the move now! And when I find out who was asleep on the watch, they're going to wish they were dead!"

"Gen—"

"Find them, fool!" Marak struck his captain with the flat side of his blade. Ignoring the stammering compliance, he grabbed Cassak by the scruff. "Now!"

"Marak." Darsal's voice cut through the purple haze in his mind.

He drew a hard breath at Darsal's gentle rebuke and let go. "Was it rebels? Or someone else?" he asked. He turned over a body. Inspected it. Recognized it as one of Eram's men.

"We're interrogating a hostage now," Cassak assured him, slightly stunned at being the brunt of his best friend's wrath. The thought crossed Marak's mind that he should apologize. But what could he say to explain the outburst?

Cassak slowly composed himself, finished his thought. "One of our men thinks he saw Warryn. Of course, if it was, the hostage won't admit it."

Sucrow.

He slammed his fist against the wall. "Sucrow, you bloody bat lover . . . !" He spun back around and got in Cassak's face, the fool captain who'd caused this mess and nearly got Darsal killed.

"Marak, we'll—"

"Get out of my sight, and get me answers," Marak growled. He shoved Cassak toward the door. "We're moving out. Now."

He swerved back around and surveyed the damage.

Darsal remained. She eyed his sword. "You want my help?"

Marak drew a breath, simmering. "I want you to pack up."

"Marak, don't be stubborn. Not now."

He sheathed his sword and started for the door.

"They're *my* friends, my general," she growled.

"You'll get yourself killed. Wait here."

"Mar—"

"I said wait here, Rona!"

Awkward silence slashed through the room.

"My name is Darsal."

His jaw tightened.

"What are you going to do?" Darsal snapped. "Storm Sucrow's temple? At least if they kill me, it's no big—"

"I need someone here," he barked. "Wait for the messenger; then find Cassak and tell him I'm going to kill that priest."

"Good riddance." Darsal followed him out the door and snaked her hand around his waist, toward his knife.

He grabbed her wrist. For a second they both stood still. All the fury drained out of him and turned to . . .

Something else. He pulled the knife toward himself, both their hands still wrapped around it. Darsal was almost touching his chest.

"Let me go with you."

Marak uncurled her fingers from the weapon and slid it into a sheath, then turned for the door. "That priest *will* kill you."

Darsal started after him again. He turned sharply, and she ran into him. He held her at arm's length. "Don't follow me."

"I have to. Elyon's orders."

Hating himself, Marak shoved her into the room and forced the door shut before she could yank it open again, then locked it.

"Post a guard," he barked at the warrior coming to his aid. "She doesn't leave. Secure the premises, and prepare to move out. And fetch me a scout."

SIX

Darsal waited until Marak was long gone. She stewed and tried not to think about what might be happening to Johnis and Silvie. Or what could possibly have caused such a fight between general and captain. This whole mess was taxing on everyone. Marak had clearly lost his mind.

Serve the mission. She loved the Horde, and she loved Marak. How loving them could help anything, how that would serve Elyon's purposes, she wasn't sure. Yet.

But Elyon made the Horde, and he loved them, wanted them, as badly as the albinos.

Finally, she could wait no longer. "You have another thing coming if you think I'm staying in here, my general."

She studied the room and took in the contents. Since the

building had never been intended for a barrack, there was little to work with.

Marak's men had sealed the windows when Johnis and Silvie were quartered here. And aside from a long candle stand or a torch, there was little in the way of weapons. And the guard wouldn't likely fall for a trick.

Darsal eyed the window, considered breaking out the bars. No, too much time.

The torches were still unlit, though. If she used one, the place would go up in flames too quickly. Instead Darsal scooted the candle stand right next to the curtains over the window, lit it, stood back, and watched them smoke.

The flame caught.

She ran for the door. "Fire!"

"LET HER ALONE," JOHNIS SNARLED. EVERYTHING WAS A HAZE. He drew a ragged breath. Silvie couldn't die. *Shaeda, help me. Together we can kill him now!*

"Entice me not," the entity growled in his ear.

"More important, you will do as I tell you, or I guarantee she won't outlive the hour." Sucrow took the knife from his servant and traced the tip along Silvie's throat. She didn't move.

Johnis saw no way out. Not with Silvie one flick of the wrist from death.

She caught his eyes and gave a slight nod, meaning for him to let her die. Let her go. Save himself, take revenge later. They could not kill the priest yet. Shaeda didn't trust herself to not kill him if she unleashed.

Johnis sagged and let out a soft groan. "Will you let her live if I promise not to defy you?" He spoke the words out loud. Of course, he still had his private thoughts of unlocking the keys to her power and keeping them—apart from her.

Darkness and fog descended, a thunderstorm on the torrent of fire. Johnis felt the abyss of failing Shaeda—her punishment, her whipping—conquer his inner rebellion.

"Josef," Silvie warned, her eyes half-closed.

Shaeda's punishment grew more insistent: Finish the mission. Regardless of cost. Even at the cost of Silvie.

Even if it meant an alliance with the priest.

"The mission holds greater weight. We require the priest's knowledge."

So she could restrain her passions, when she chose. Her hate she held at bay, knowing the result of the mission would bring far greater satisfaction than killing him now to save Silvie.

"Only as long as you do as you're told." Sucrow played with the blade resting against Silvie's neck. Revulsion snaked down Johnis's spine, twisting his face in disgust. Of course the priest would think Johnis was talking to him.

"Be careful what you wish for," Silvie whispered, pulling away from the priest, her voice low and devoid of emotion.

The door burst open. Darsal stood on the threshold, wielding a long silver candle stand, her cowl once more over her face.

Sucrow curled his lip. "Stay out of this, albino."

She came between Johnis and Sucrow, inching toward the altar. Johnis took advantage of the slave's entrance and managed to stagger to his feet with his arms at his sides.

The albino joined Sucrow at the altar. She hesitated with her makeshift club.

"Put that down," Sucrow ordered the slave. His hand opened, palm stretched out toward her, fingers curled. Darsal was suddenly flung against the wall. Her weapon clattered to the ground. She didn't move.

A guard went for her.

Shaeda, we have to get out of here. Now.

Johnis drew a sharp breath. "I will take you there, and I will do what you will. But if you kill her, I will come after you." He met Sucrow's eyes. "And then I will kill you."

"You're hardly in a position to make threats."

Sucrow nicked Silvie's throat to make his point. Her blood oozed along her soft skin and onto the altar. The priest collected the crimson liquid onto his fingers and dipped them into a bowl of water.

"It's always more fun through the throat."

Sucrow poured the bowl's contents onto the wound. Smoke curled, sizzling. Silvie yelped and tried to jerk away but had nowhere to go.

The priest kept pouring. Silvie's skin turned from white to yellow-green to gray.

Johnis lunged, but the guards held him back by the wrists. "Leave her alone!"

"It won't kill her. At least, it isn't supposed to." Sucrow cackled.

A flash of movement. Darsal lifted the candle stand and went for the priest. Swung. Sucrow barely dodged the blow and dropped his bowl, reeling backward. Darsal jumped between Silvie and the priest.

Sucrow stood. He opened his palm and unleashed a stream of fire. Darsal dodged as the flame grazed her shoulder and scorched the stone floor. Her body slapped against the rock, her head bouncing.

Sucrow glided to Silvie's side, amused at the whole situation. "Or perhaps I could do worse." He dug his nails into her cheek. Silvie growled but could do nothing. The bloodstain taunted Johnis.

The priest kissed his fingers.

Johnis's chest constricted. His muscles curled into knots. Shaeda—or he—snarled.

As Darsal groaned and picked herself up off the floor, Sucrow threw his knife at her. But another knife whizzed through the air and struck the priest's midflight. The weapons ricocheted off each other and skittered across the hard floor. A blast of sound. Darsal slammed back against the wall, away from Johnis. Sucrow's sorcery.

The room went still.

General Marak of Southern stood on the threshold, another knife ready. His gray-white eyes homed in on the priest.

"I'm pleased you could join us, General," Sucrow scoffed, turning.

Johnis could feel the changes as Shaeda's power finally began to flow into him. His heart pounded. They would end this, ally with the priest, get the general and the albino out of the way. His fists knotted. He could snap the metal chains like twigs.

"You're well out of line, Priest," Marak growled.

"She's just an albino."

"Arya is not. Release them now. We're getting this cursed expedition over with."

Johnis lunged for Silvie, but Marak caught him by the collar. Shaeda—through Johnis—lifted her hand and raised it toward Sucrow. She began to recite in a language Johnis didn't know. His heart rate spiked.

"Save it," the general snapped. "The next time, Priest, I will kill you."

Sucrow cackled. "I half expected you to go running for Qurong."

Marak's eyes narrowed. "More proof I am not a priest. Let the girl up. We don't have time for this."

Inside him, Shaeda stirred, acknowledged the shift in focus. She lowered her talon and stopped mid-incantation. Marak was not in defiance of the priest; neither would he allow the priest access to the amulet. They were working together. He felt her power ebb. There would be no snapping of the chains.

Shaeda, please!

Johnis tugged his shackles. Didn't Shaeda care?

No, not as long as he was not in danger. Marak was now the mediator between this entity inside and the priest. As long as it furthered the mission, she would not interfere. He must endure a little longer.

"And if I choose not to?" Sucrow sneered.

"Then Josef and I make the expedition without you." The general's expression darkened.

No! Silvie!

Johnis dove for one of Marak's knives. Marak drew back and slapped him to the ground, hard. Johnis started up, but Marak's sword point threatened to run him through.

"Enough," Marak snarled. "What are your terms, Priest?"

Sucrow considered his options. "I keep the girl until this is over."

"Fine. If she dies, the agreement is breached."

"Agreed. And you kill the albino. She attacked me."

The two stared each other down.

Marak pulled Johnis up and let him stand, but kept a knife pressed against his ribs. "Come," he ordered Johnis and Darsal. "We have preparations to make."

SEVEN

Sucrow left his servants to clean up the mess and load the girl into a small cart with a built-in cage for transport. She would be ready along with his other provisions. He went to take a final look at the old legends, at the ceremony. It had been there all along, right under his nose. He chided himself for not seeing these things before.

But soon enough he would no longer require these fools.

Perhaps by then Marak would be in line. If not . . . more drastic measures might be required. But what more could you do to a man once you'd stripped him of everything?

Well, not everything. Marak still had his position and his very prominent ego.

And his life. And his best friend, Cassak.

But his beloved captain would soon be leaving him. The mere

thought made Sucrow laugh. Already the potion was doing its work. Loyalties could be bought, coerced, and traded for improved honor.

"My lord?"

Sucrow glanced up, scowling. A servant stood at the door. Upon his bidding the wretch approached and bowed low.

"What could possibly lead you to bother me at this hour?"

"Marak's captain is here."

Like a faithful dog. Sucrow chuckled.

"Bring him in."

Sounds of commotion filtered in from the hallway as the captain stalked in, sword half-slung. His face was tight, shoulders back. Sucrow couldn't quite read his expression.

"Reconsidered so soon, Captain?" Sucrow asked.

Cassak's eyes turned icy. "What is it you want of me?"

Sucrow sat forward and laced his fingers beneath his chin. So the fish had taken the bait, had he? He concentrated, summoning the power of his lord and master to his aid. The captain scratched a spot on his neck, uncomfortable. He could not see the little serpent with its red, pulsing, star-shaped eye at his own throat.

So simple, this ability to control the heart and mind and body of a man.

"Nothing too difficult," Sucrow assured. "You executed Jordan of Southern along with the other two, correct?"

The captain answered slowly. "I did."

Technically true. Cassak carried out Marak's order. It didn't really matter. Marak was there; Marak gave the order. Sucrow just needed the general to remember who let fly the arrow.

"I would like a copy of your report, as well as Marak's notations and Martyn's war journals." At Cassak's hesitation, Sucrow reminded, "Qurong gave the general and me equal standing. He did not relinquish my rights to oversee executions. Besides, my understanding is the general made copies. I merely wish to see one of them."

"Why do you want it now?"

"Merely review." Sucrow managed something close to a pleased look. He took his staff in hand. "There is no need to tell Marak. I also want the amulet."

"That doesn't answer my question."

"Patience, Captain. Tell me something: do you enjoy being a captain? I will put in a word to Qurong that your services have not yet been rewarded. What do you think?"

The little snake bit the captain on the jaw, entrancing him.

Cassak didn't answer, but his eyes said he was interested.

"Together we will remind Marak of his duties."

MARAK STOOD IN THE CLEARING SOUTH OF MIDDLE, JUST beyond the gates. His commanders flocked around him. Everyone was accounted for save Sucrow, Darsal, and Josef. He half listened to his commanders, who all parroted things he already knew.

Teeleh's breath, since when had he become so irritable with his own men?

Darsal had slipped away. He didn't like the albino being where he couldn't see her. Where had she gone?

"General, the priest and his men are unaware—"

"A warrior is prepared to break camp and run in under five minutes," Marak said. Sucrow would show up, just as planned. If the old priest moved too slow and had to catch up, so be it. "We're leaving as soon as the scouts report."

He reviewed the checklist in silence. Cassak was supposed to meet up with him in the desert and signal his men to follow . . . provided he didn't make any more mistakes. He'd become intolerable since his return, since the Eramite skirmish.

And spending so much time on his own . . .

"General, are you certain this is wise?"

"Are you afraid of a superstitious old man, Commander?"

Pause.

"No, sir. It's only—"

Marak passed his checklist to the commanders to mark off. "What makes a warrior, Reyan?"

The man snapped to attention. "Loyalty, integrity, honesty, sir."

"Shall I think less of my officers, Commander Reyan?"

"No, sir."

At his look the men scattered to their final preparations. Marak turned on his heel, scanning the shoreline. The priest would come. It was only a matter of time. He bit back a mocking laugh.

He didn't wait much longer before Warryn, chief of the Throaters, came riding hard through the forest. Warryn swung down. Marak noticed he wore an eye patch now.

So the Throater's blunder had cost him his eye; Sucrow was a harsh master.

"The priest wants to know why you're leaving without him."

Marak shrugged. "I'm ready to leave. Or do priests not move as swiftly as warriors?"

"He's on his way," Warryn persisted. A smug look crossed his face, as if he knew something Marak didn't. "He's sent me ahead to ensure you do not leave."

"We don't have the time for games."

Warryn's expression sobered. "It has to do with the expedition, General. I'm sure he has his reasons."

"He is aware we're on a schedule, is he not?"

One blank, cold eye drilled him, then shifted to Darsal, who had just appeared through the clearing. Darsal glared back at him, then turned her attention to Marak. She touched the Circle pendant around her neck.

Warryn made a sound in the back of his throat. "The priest wishes also to know when you plan to kill the slave."

"Excuse me?"

"Are you doing it yourself, or will you have another perform the execution?"

Marak snapped his head up. His hand brushed his hilt. This Throater would never touch Darsal. A fleeting thought crossed his mind, that Cassak had asked the same question. He dismissed it.

"Concern yourself with the present, not the future, Throater. I'll kill her when I'm done punishing her."

The gloat on Warryn's face shriveled to a blank, wide-eyed stare. Then his eye narrowed and darkened.

"Respectfully, General, the future and the present are not so distant from one another. What occurs in one will affect the other by design."

Someone cleared his throat. Reyan. His ranking commander rubbed a spot on his ear, not quite shaking his head, and made brief eye contact.

"Tell Sucrow we need to move out quickly," Reyan said to the Throater. "There's no time to waste."

Warryn's face tightened.

"Now."

The Throater gave one look at Marak, who nodded, and took his leave.

Reyan waited.

Marak relaxed his fist.

Reyan nodded pointedly toward the trees. "We brought in a dozen albinos, General."

More albinos? They were getting harder to find by the day. "Where?"

"More of Jordan of Southern's brood. Apparently the Eramites drove them out. We await your command to execute them."

A test. Only Cassak would be so bold as to test Marak by forcing him to order an execution just to see if he would do it. He must have set this up so Reyan would have to ask. The captain was making a point to the men. And to his general. Since when did Cassak question Marak's abilities?

Something was wrong. He'd never been so angry with his friend in his life, and never had Cassak had cause or desire to doubt him. It all started with Jordan and Rona, didn't it?

Or . . . did it?

Reyan cleared his throat. "General?"

On instinct he checked his pocket for the medallion. It was . . . gone.

Marak snarled. "Execute them."

He stalked off without waiting for a reply, grabbing Darsal by the scruff on the way and dragging her off into the trees.

EIGHT

E*lyon, why is he manhandling me? The fire?*

Marak glanced over his shoulder. He loomed over her. Close. So close . . .

"Where's the amulet? Are you trying to ruin me?" He straightened and turned toward her, his eyes drilling her. He wanted her to say it. To admit it.

Darsal couldn't help but feel startled. Marak fully expected nothing but the truth from her. An albino. Had she made so much progress?

She crossed her arms and looked Marak in the eye. She didn't know what Marak was talking about. For all she knew this was a ruse so he could say he'd already interrogated her before conducting his real search. Her sense of vengeance flared over the condemned albinos, equally met with the utter despair of his deception and the shocking revelation of his trust.

Her mind caught up. She couldn't save the albinos. She could keep this thread of trust. "You want the truth."

Marak's arms folded over his chest. Her heart skipped a beat. Did he really trust her so much? The general was so close. And now—now everything seemed to hinge on her answer.

She drew a breath. Let his newfound trust in her sink in. "I didn't take the amulet, my general."

His fist curled. "Someone did."

"It wasn't me. Ask your captain."

"Cassak is my best friend," he said. But his eyes betrayed doubt. Marak considered his albino slave more trustworthy than his Scab captain now?

Darsal backed off. Marak was irrational when it came to those close to him. Irrational enough to accuse his best friend of stealing from him. "It still wasn't me."

"And the fire?"

"I just needed out of the room. I wasn't trying to burn the place to the ground."

And for that she thought he might either break down or explode.

"Neither Josef nor Sucrow has it?"

Marak cleared his throat. "Both claim innocence. My guess is the bloody priest, but he's got someone else holding it."

"You want me to steal it from him?"

He didn't answer immediately. For a full minute she stared at his back. She started to reach for his arm, but he turned back around.

"In the lair, if something were to happen, you wouldn't be able to run."

Her brow furrowed. Surely he didn't think her a coward. She studied his eyes. No, no, it was something else. "Now, there's a change of subject."

"I can handle the priest," he said.

He had not answered her question. Silent affirmation? Denial?

Marak withdrew something small and silver from his pocket, then stooped and reached for her leg. Darsal jerked. Kicked, out of habit. Marak stilled, and something in his expression twisted. With an uneven breath, Darsal willed herself to relax.

"What are you doing?" she demanded.

Her general lifted her foot to his knee and unlocked the shackle. He then did the same with the other. For a moment he stayed there, kneeling with her sandaled foot on his knee, key and open shackle in his hands. Darsal suddenly felt silly.

Marak was . . . releasing her?

He straightened and set her foot on the ground.

And then she was alone.

Marak's voice bellowed across the clearing at his men. A few horses whinnied. The breeze sent a chill through her, despite the warm sun.

Her feet felt so light after wearing the heavy chain. Now . . .

now all was weightless and surreal. Even the ground beneath her barely seemed to touch her. Dare she think she had Marak's heart?

Dare she think she could keep it?

Tree branches swayed gently, leaves rustling. Instinctively she looked up, hoping for a flicker of white wings.

"What will you do?"

Darsal swung around, dropped to a crouch.

Gabil was in front of her. "You could leave, you know. He would understand."

"I don't know what you mean." That idea stung her. It wasn't part of her mission. Elyon's mission.

"Yes, you do."

Darsal straightened her shoulders. "I can't leave without Johnis and Silvie. Without Marak."

"They've chosen their paths."

"They're in pain."

"Yes. They are. They are deceived."

"You would have me leave them like this?" She didn't believe what she was hearing. Gabil wanted her to scrap the mission?

"You cannot save them all, Darsal."

Indignation filled her. The Horde was as worth saving as the Circle, and save them she would. Or die trying.

"I only want to save three. Why do you want me to run to safety? If I leave, I condemn them. I condemn the Circle."

"That is true."

Darsal didn't answer. *Gabil isn't telling me to leave them. He's showing me why I have to stay.*

"Love him for Elyon, Darsal. For Johnis."

She balked. The hair on the back of her neck rose. It was a thread of hope, but it hinged on her ability to love a Scab general.

And on his returning that love.

"Darsal!" Marak's voice bellowed from the clearing, through the grove of trees. They were ready to leave.

Gabil flapped off.

"Darsal?" Marak came through the trees, sighted her. Stopped.

She raised her chin. Stood in front of him just as she had that day in the dungeon. Looking at him, the fight left her. In its place was deep sorrow and love.

"I'm here."

Marak looked at her gravely with an expression she'd never seen. And she knew: he'd expected her to leave.

For a moment they stared at each other. And then it was over.

Marak turned back into the stoic warrior and started back for the others. "It's time to leave."

NIGHT FELL OVER THE EXPEDITION PARTY. SERVANTS CARRYing long torches surrounded their masters, creating a ring of fire against the starlit night. The desert cooled with the rising moon. Johnis rode ahead, Sucrow and Marak behind and to either side of him. Out on the wings, two commanders. He'd noticed some strange activity between Cassak and Sucrow but thought little of it. Cassak was a mediating figure—it was likely all usual. Marak either didn't notice or wasn't disturbed by his captain's movements.

Behind them all, servants . . . followed by the Throaters. They cut south through the canyons, past Natalga Gap, and into the endless sand.

Silvie should be riding next to him, not held captive by an evil priest and caged at the tail of the procession. He had to think of a way to free Silvie. He had to . . .

The siren song swelled, overpowered his vision so he could no longer think of Silvie. Johnis felt his senses sharpen and his focus narrow. He could think only of the mission.

Shaeda.

You are beautiful, he thought. *Tell me more. You are a queen, with a mate, yet the Leedhan were not born until after the Desecration.*

She gave a low, seductive laugh. *"You are correct, my fair one, I am the eldest of our kind, at eighteen. Does such please you, that one so young might wield such power?"*

He didn't have time to answer.

"I see nothing," Sucrow growled. He clutched his staff. A strange, heady sensation fell over them.

The moon rose high into the east now, and Johnis turned his horse to confront the broad length of shadow, moon at his back.

"Patience, Priest," Marak snapped. His irises were enormous, or his pupils had shrunk strangely.

"I think we've shown more than enough patience for the time being, General."

"How far until we turn west?" Marak demanded. His mood had gone from irritable to completely foul. Now he seemed to struggle with something, but Johnis couldn't pinpoint it.

The siren song distracted him. Shaeda's mind was open to Johnis once more. She gave him instruction as they traveled. The further they went, the more he saw through multicolored Leedhan eyes.

"Not much farther. Another hour or so, I think."

Marak humphed his answer. "We'll need to make camp, then."

"Camp?"

"You didn't expect to ride through the night, did you?"

"It's a long way. I thought you were all in a hurry."

Shaeda's song spurred him along. She was fantasizing as much as she was planning their next move, seeing farther ahead than anyone could have realized.

These miserable fools made of clay had no idea what was coming for them.

Marak had been taking stock of the area. Shaeda's gaze lingered on the general for a long moment. Johnis could make nothing of her assessment. Her thoughts were growing more guarded, more cautious.

"Here's as good a place as any," Marak said.

"Continue on . . ."

"We should continue," Shaeda said. Johnis said.

"There is nothing." Johnis said, his voice hard and clipped. "Not until we reach the canyon. We should keep going."

Marak dismounted. "Ten minutes." Silvie refused Sucrow's assistance down and nearly fell off the horse, trying to dismount.

Silvie had refused to look at Johnis as she was forced into a cage. Johnis considered how to rescue her while Marak, the officers, and Sucrow went to discuss whatever it was that Marak wanted to discuss.

Silvie . . .

Shaeda clamped down, her rival now out of the way.

Johnis stumbled off his horse and sank to the ground, elbows on his knees. He rubbed his temples. Against Shaeda's wishes, the caravan had stopped.

"*We must not linger, my pet.*" Her claws cut into him.

"I can't control him," he protested under his breath. "I can't. There's no telling the blasted general what to do. Patience, please."

He was punished every time someone else slowed her down. Shaeda's invisible grip tightened.

"Let me go," he whispered. He couldn't see. He couldn't think.

She was crushing him, squeezing the life out of him. Her will, her mind, her heart, her thoughts—her loves and hates—all his. And his were hers. *Silvie . . .*

Shaeda suddenly relented. She chuckled. *You are correct, my pet, my little human . . . Leave such obstacles to me.*

Johnis struggled for air. He opened his eyes and sat up. Brushed dust off his arms.

"Johnis?"

Johnis's head shot up. Darsal stood beneath a desert tree, an overgrown piece of white bark and shriveled branches that thrived with cacti growing from it. He tensed. Darsal came closer. He could smell her raw, pungent skin even through the citrusy fragrance she was wearing. He curled his lip and showed her his back.

"What should we do?" he whispered. He watched the others, waiting for Shaeda's insight to overtake him.

"Elyon, Johnis."

Shaeda bared their teeth and growled. "Elyon abandoned us, wench!" He spun, close enough to smell her sickly sweet breath.

And then he saw Marak wasn't making camp. Instead he was preparing to speak with his officers and Sucrow. If he could get to Silvie . . .

"Patience, Johnis. She shall be returned. But she is needed to convince the albino to stand down."

What do you mean? It was Darsal, after all . . .

And then, for the moment, Shaeda was gone. At least, he didn't sense her. That could change.

"Why don't you focus on killing Sucrow, not the Circle?"

"Sucrow." The name drew bile from deep within. He glanced over at the priest's caravan, where Silvie was.

Darsal's eyes followed his. "We don't have long, Johnis. Back out. Silvie needs you to drown."

"What?" He withdrew from her. Was she mad?

Darsal started over. "No, listen. The red pools—You need to drown in them. It's the only way. It's—"

"The heat's gotten to you."

She grabbed his arm.

Johnis pulled free. Drown. Murderous albino wench. His lip curled. "Leave me."

Her brow arched. "Is that you or the entity talking?"

The Leedhan's eyes homed in on Darsal. Darsal could drop dead.

"Distract the guard," the albino said. "We can save Silvie from the priest." Her eyes flicked to the officers and Sucrow.

His eyes narrowed. "Why should I trust an albino?"

"Because the albino is the only other person who cares about Silvie." Darsal crossed her arms. "And because I think your answer will help you determine where your heart's going. But decidc. I don't have all night."

Johnis struggled for control. His heart . . . He was following his heart, wasn't he? Or . . . was he?

His heart was with Silvie. As long as he didn't thwart the mission . . .

Shaeda, Shaeda, don't tell me one woman can thwart the mission. Just give me this.

The Leedhan didn't like the idea. No, she wouldn't. Silvie had his heart, which meant his entity did not.

If Darsal dies, it doesn't hinder the mission. What's the harm?

"I need an answer, Johnis. They'll move out any minute."

Shaeda finally relented. As long as this didn't interfere. The priest and the general must remain allies, must continue this fool's quest.

They were so naive . . .

Johnis gave Darsal a sharp nod. "Let's go."

NINE

Darsal left Johnis and stole through groups of Throaters and warriors who waited while their leaders convened. A waning moon gave her just enough light to see by. Guards skirted the perimeter of the band of Horde while the officers and Sucrow spoke in private. The light from a few torches broke through the shadows.

She could still barely wrap her mind around the fact that Johnis was being controlled by a Leedhan. And she felt guilty about the ruse of going after Silvie—she didn't need Johnis's help, and chances were slim she'd be able to aid Silvie. But if she could get Johnis to think, maybe, just maybe . . . he'd forgive her in the end, once he saw she'd only meant to steer his attention away from the Leedhan.

Silvie would be more than willing to be rid of the priest and to help Johnis with the amulet. Still . . . that did nothing for the nagging in the back of Darsal's mind. She passed by the outcropping of rock where Marak and the others were still meeting. They were mildly secluded, yet still in the open. Darsal dodged a couple of servants. Marak's voice sounded strained, furious about something. But he didn't yell. He kept his voice low—a soft, chilling sound.

Darsal inched toward the canvas-covered cage on wheels, where Silvie was being held, then caught herself. She hugged the shadows. Two Throaters stood guard. One could be Warryn.

She waited for Johnis, who said something to the guard to draw his attention away. The guard hesitated. Johnis grew persistent. At last the guard grumbled and followed Johnis.

Good. The scrapper was still there, inside his flaking shell—somewhere.

Darsal looked both ways, climbed up, and ducked inside. Incense filled her nose and mouth. She coughed and stumbled over something.

A muffled voice. Far corner. Darsal's heart nearly stopped. *Silvie.*

Hating herself, Darsal inched around and started a sweep for the medallion. If Sucrow had left it, she could get it. She'd rather Silvie not know she was here.

Darsal heard a low groan. Silvie was hurting. Time was running out. She heard voices. Rummaged faster.

Love them, Darsal. Love them.

"Stay away from me," Silvie groaned.

Darsal froze. Silvie was looking straight at her. Darsal started to speak, then thought better of it. What could she say? She climbed over Sucrow's meager supplies, trying not to gag on the smell of the incense.

She saw a bag, reached for it. Started to dig. "What happened, Silvie?"

Icy silence.

Reaching deep into the bag, Darsal felt something cool and round. The medallion. So the rat *had* managed to somehow get it from Marak. Interesting. Who took it? Warryn, perhaps?

Or was Sucrow working some magic? If that were the case, he could have made Marak give it to him himself, and Marak wouldn't necessarily remember a thing.

Frustrated, she shoved it in her pocket and stood. Glanced at Silvie. Her hands and ankles were tied, and she was lying on her stomach on the wood. She was bruised and had a nasty gash on her neck. She glared, then turned her head away.

"Sil—"

Movement. When she turned to the door, two Throaters stood there, torches in one hand, swords in the other. One wore an eye patch.

Warryn.

"Looking for something?" the Throater sneered.

Where was Johnis?

Darsal scanned the tent for a weapon. "Orders," she snapped.

"Really? Marak's?" Warryn spat.

"It isn't your concern." She raised a brow. "What should be

your concern is what will happen when Marak discovers you holding me at sword point."

A gentle, invisible tug reprimanded her. Love Warryn too? He was Horde, wasn't he? No. Not Warryn. Marak was one thing, but this monster . . .

Warryn snorted. "What does Marak care about an albino?"

Darsal chose her answer carefully. "I should ask him for you." She raised a brow. "You want me to ask him?"

The Throater didn't quite know what to do with that. She got a good look at him. Sucrow had taken his eye. Now the quiet sorrow poured in. Elyon, they were all so deceived . . .

No time.

"Let me pass." She started forward.

Warryn caught her at the door. Yanked her back by the hair. His sword touched her throat. "What did you take?"

"Kill me and find out." Darsal lifted her chin. Her heart pounded. Elyon might not want her to harm this Scab, but she was about to have no alternative. "I'm under orders not to talk. What do you make of that?"

"Whose orders?"

"Are you deaf? Let me pass, or I'll take your other eye out."

Warryn hesitated.

Darsal ducked free of the blade. He barely missed her neck. She somersaulted, landed on her feet, and ran for the other tents. Servants scattered. She grabbed one and flung him in Warryn's direction.

Several more Throaters came after her.

She ran for open desert, slid down the far side of a dune, letting the sand cover her. Darsal held her breath.

"DARSAL! SILVIE!" JOHNIS'S HUSHED WHISPER ECHOED OVER the dunes. Shaeda overpowered him, made him stagger like a drunk.

"The albino betrayed you," Shaeda kept insisting. *"Seek her not . . . Your mate is yet within the priest's claws; resist no further."*

"Her name is *Silvie*, you bloody vampire!" Johnis continued his search. Darsal would have hidden out here someplace, away from the chaos their ruse had created.

She'd used him. The bloody albino had used him. He'd find her and—

Darsal, covered in sand, came out of hiding to face him. He drew his sword, ready for the kill, but Shaeda was there . . .

He was vaguely aware of Darsal speaking to him, saying his name. But before his eyes she became Shaeda. Slender fingers with clawlike nails tipped his chin up. He shuddered at the rush of power the contact sent roaring through his veins.

Tasty, like copper and salt.

"Johnis." He knew Darsal was talking to him. Knew she'd come out of the sand dunes and stood in front of him. But he *saw* the Leedhan.

Her long, white-gold hair spilled over her shoulders like a

wedding veil. Perfectly smooth skin, so delicate a scratch might break through to the veins. A seductive smile spread across her face. Her haunting gaze drank him in.

"Johnis, I had to do it," Darsal was saying. "I had to get the amulet back from Sucrow. I wasn't trying to cheat you, I promise."

"Look upon me, my pet." Shaeda's fingertips traced his throat, his jaw, his lips.

He found his voice. "You have more than enough power to free her."

"Power?" Darsal scoffed. "I am a slave, Johnis." Her eyes widened as she realized he hadn't meant her. The Leedhan had him in her grasp. "Let him be."

"All in time. I will not abandon you." Shaeda stroked his cheek. The heavy, oppressive darkness bore down on his mind. His body tensed. Senses heightened.

Shaeda and he were one.

"She means no harm," Johnis said. Shaeda said. Did he really believe that? Did it matter? "She guides and protects me. She loves me."

"She'll use and kill you," Darsal warned.

Shaeda embraced him. Her iron grip held him fast. Her scent and gaze overwhelmed him. She kissed him. Hard and long. Needlelike teeth pinched his lip. She . . . bit him. Blood trickled from the small puncture.

"Silvie loves you, Johnis. So does Elyon. Even I do, when you aren't being foolish." Darsal, not Shaeda.

The Leedhan nipped him again. Johnis tried to turn his head and pull out of her kiss, but her slender arms and lithe body held him fast. When she finally drew back, a small drop of his blood glittered on her eerie white skin. Johnis licked his lips and tasted salt and iron.

Her mind opened to him once more.

"Johnis!" Darsal slapped him, hard, and grabbed him by the tunic. Her dark eyes met his. "Listen to me."

Shaeda couldn't be kissing him, could she? It was just another mirage, another illusion to control him . . .

His lip curled. Shaeda hissed. "Give me the amulet!"

Darsal drew back, scowling. Shaeda grabbed at her. Darsal slashed Johnis's arm with her fingernails and darted free. Shaeda's power poured into him. He would kill her.

No, he didn't want to kill Darsal, did he?

"Grab me like that again," Darsal warned, "and I'll give the amulet right back to the priest."

Shaeda snarled. She—Johnis—lunged for Darsal again. The albino grabbed Johnis's wrist and slammed him into the sand.

"Johnis, stop it!"

He was on his feet in a second and dove for Darsal's throat. She dodged. Shaeda pounced.

Johnis struggled hard. He was mad at her, but he didn't want to kill her, did he? Shaeda squeezed him, breathing threats. His vision went black.

A white wing soared past their heads. Shaeda shrieked and jumped back. Johnis's gaze shot skyward. A Roush!

She feared Roush as well? His entity slammed the door shut on all thought.

Darsal snatched the amulet from where it had fallen. She turned and ran toward the officers before the Leedhan could recover.

"You fool!" Shaeda snapped.

Embracing Shaeda's wrath, Johnis bared his teeth. Silvie was still with the priest. He'd kill that albino.

TEN

"Gabil, thank Elyon," Darsal whispered as she ran. The Roush darted around her shoulders, soundlessly following her. Torchlight settled over rock and sand, turning both orange and yellow. Smoke drifted around the warriors. Marak and his men were still meeting. She crept forward.

"Try not to do anything foolish," Gabil whispered back, worried. "There is no sense in you getting killed, although you might have assisted Silvie while you were at it. I daresay you'd be best off destroying that thing."

"There wasn't time. And I don't have a choice. Marak will be in a world of trouble if something happens." Gabil didn't answer. "Besides, I can't love him if I'm dead."

"You've a point."

Sucrow said something she couldn't hear. He sounded low and dark, a serpent on the hunt. Darsal's skin prickled.

"Leave her out of this," Marak barked back. "My private life is not your concern."

Sucrow laughed. Spoke clearly. "You're still in love with a dead albino, aren't you?"

Metal sang from a scabbard.

"Put that away, General."

"If I can execute my brother, Priest," Marak said evenly, "what do you think I can do to you?" Technicality. Marak gave the order. Cassak carried it out. Marak, true to his word, had stood watch. But giving the order was the same thing as doing it, really.

Seconds ticked by. Then Sucrow stormed away, seething.

Darsal ducked behind him. She pressed her hands along the rock. Gabil flapped off before anyone could spot him. Marak still stood with his sword half-drawn.

The general let it slide back into its scabbard when he saw her. "What did you do? Warryn came barging over here and—"

Darsal reached into her pocket. "I stole something." She held the medallion where he could see it.

His scowl deepened. Brow furrowed. His foul mood from the meeting with Sucrow was souring fast. "Priest and his magic," he grumbled. "Where was it?" he asked Darsal.

"Sucrow's things. He lied to you."

"Sucrow's . . ." He glared. Reached for the medallion.

His big, calloused fingers brushed hers. Warm and rough.

Electrifying.

He paused there, with the medallion half in his hand, half in hers. He was glowering at her, but behind the anger was something else . . .

The spell broke. He took the amulet. "I told you to stay out of this," he snapped.

"It was worth the risk, don't you think?" She raised a brow. "Or don't you want that? You know, maybe I should have given it back to Josef. He'd like that." She reached for the medallion. He pulled it out of her reach.

"That was careless." Marak shut his eyes and took several breaths.

"He'd like Arya back too. Or would you rob him of his lover as the priest did you?"

The general grew still for a long moment. Then tried to brush past her. She was pushing. Too far and she would run counter to her own mission.

"Move."

"Marak." Darsal put her hand on his wrist and drew closer. "Josef won't rest until Arya is as far away from Sucrow as possible. I would think you of all people would know what the priest can do."

"My duty is to Qurong, Darsal." He tried to go around her again, but she planted herself in front of him. "What makes you think Sucrow will hurt Josef's girl?"

"What makes you think he won't?" She wound her hands around each of his wrists. "Why are you being so bullheaded?"

Marak stared at her, half-irritated, half-relenting. He didn't trust the priest, and they both knew it. "She was part of the deal."

She threw him a dirty look.

He drew a heavy breath and pulled his arms out of her grasp.

"Dars—" He'd started to yell, but caught himself. "I'll handle the priest."

"Thank you. Josef and I would appreciate that."

He gave her a long look. "Do you really think I want that girl hurt?"

"I think your sense of duty overpowers your common sense." Darsal quirked a brow. "I think Jordan likely thought the same."

"Why do you keep bringing him up?"

She glanced over her shoulder and lowered her voice. "Because sometimes I think that's the only way I can get through to you."

Marak slid past her and went back to the expedition party. Darsal watched him, panged with guilt. Elyon wouldn't like her being this way with him, losing the ground she'd already gained. Even losing his heart. She drew a breath, knew she had to . . .

"Well, that didn't go well."

She turned. Gabil was perched on the rock.

"You're going to let him leave like that?"

"I was on my way." She glared at him. "I swear he's going to be the death of me."

Gabil fell quiet a second. "Hopefully not. He's deceived, though. You have to remember that."

"Deceived, not stupid." Darsal crossed her arms.

"He's killed his brother and his lover, and he isn't allowed to even mourn them, daughter."

She softened. "So what do I do? Now he and Johnis are both mad at me."

"Surely you didn't need Johnis to steal the amulet from Sucrow."

A pang of guilt. "It was easier. And I thought . . . I thought it would help him see things properly."

"Did you?"

Darsal looked to the side. No, she hadn't. She just knew she had to get the amulet from Sucrow, and Johnis would help her get it if Silvie were involved.

"Love comes naturally for humans. Stop making it difficult."

Her general called out to her.

She glanced back, conceded the Roush's point. "When will I see you again?"

Gabil smiled. "When Elyon pleases."

She grabbed the torch and hurried back, caught Marak's tunic before he'd gone far. He stopped, but didn't turn.

"Marak, I'm . . . I'm sorry." Darsal came around in front of him, still holding the torch. The light caught his eyes, and suddenly she wondered what color they would be. What color his skin would be.

He looked so haggard, so worn by all of this. The general was exhausted, physically, emotionally, mentally. Her heart ached for him.

Marak gave her a long look, eyes softening. He started to answer; then his gaze shot over her shoulder. Darsal looked. Cassak was coming. She could almost feel the captain and general turning cold.

Something had definitely happened.

"General," Cassak said with a curt nod. His eyes looked strange. Darsal studied him. Funny, she thought she saw the snake tattoo on his neck, with a star-shaped eye.

"Eyes to see," Gabil whispered from somewhere.

Her eyes widened. Elyon was showing her something. Someone had gotten to the captain—and changed him.

Marak folded his arms. "Captain. The priest somehow got ahold of the amulet. I'd like to know how."

Cassak's eyes narrowed. He responded slowly. "I'll find out. The commanders are ready to move out when you are."

"I'm ready now."

Cassak saluted and turned to leave. Marak grabbed Cassak's forearm and brought his face close to the side of his captain's head.

"Provided nothing else goes missing."

The captain's expression hardened. "I'll see to it, General." Marak let him go, and Cassak was dismissed.

Darsal studied Marak, who was staring after his childhood friend. "You think he took it?"

Marak answered slowly. "I think I put nothing past the priest."

"The priest, no . . . but . . ." She barely knew the man and could barely fathom the thought. Still, she saw what she saw, and her heart ached all the more for her general.

"Nothing is for certain, Darsal. Nothing." Marak's voice was cool. "Let's go."

A THOUSAND POSSIBILITIES FOR RESCUING SILVIE PRESENTED themselves, and Shaeda denied him every one. Her presence settled hard over Johnis, the blue-purple haze tinting the torches held by the warriors' servants.

The commanders rode and ordered the questing party to fall in line. Once more a ring of torches surrounded the main party. Beyond, Cassak and his hundred men guarded them from Eramites, jackals, albinos, and anything else they might encounter.

Marak loped back to the head alongside Johnis. "Ride."

Johnis glowered, prepared to invoke Shaeda. Then he saw Sucrow sneering at him, and his blood ran cold. Silvie . . .

He scanned the group. He glimpsed Silvie by one of the horses, bound, face bloody and whiter than usual. Something clear oozed between the cracks in her skin.

"What did you do to Arya?"

Shaeda's talons dug into him.

"That's for me to know." Sucrow leered and licked his lips.

Shaeda, through Johnis, stared down Sucrow.

"Priest." Marak's harsh voice interrupted, an edge in it not present before. "Enough."

He couldn't get Silvie's attention . . . or she wasn't going to look at him. Shaeda's mind opened to him, honing his focus on baiting the Shataiki guardian queen. This was the final stretch.

A stray thought: *Why are they called "queens"? There's no gender with Shataiki. It's confusing.*

Shaeda turned coy. *"Shataiki thrive on confusion, my pet."*

"Josef?" Darsal spoke to him from his right. Why couldn't she just let him be? She probed him with deceptively warm brown eyes.

"Mind your own business." Johnis tried to mount.

She grabbed the reins.

Johnis pushed past her. "We finish the mission."

A long stare. "Sucrow doesn't care either." She let him go and went to catch up to the general before Johnis could shove her in the dirt.

Johnis took his place at the head of the group, Shaeda guiding them with him as mediator.

Never in a million years will I be like that inhuman priest.

ELEVEN

Dawn broke over the horizon, turning the desert pink and orange. On and on south they rode, past carrion birds and cacti. She'd heard jackals through the night, but thankfully, never saw them.

Darsal couldn't stop twisting around in her saddle and swinging her legs like a child as Johnis—Josef—turned their course west. She would be lucky to accomplish anything more than a free trip to the nuthouse at this rate. Her thoughts centered on what to do next, how to stop the tide.

She sagged forward in her saddle and rode on, separated from the others by every means possible. Thirty minutes passed, then an hour.

Half-consciously, Darsal spurred her horse and rode out to circle and look for any sign of danger. She drove her horse on, seeing nothing but the occasional flicker that could have been Cassak's men, Eram's men, or a bat of either variety.

Marak called after her, but she wasn't ready to acknowledge him yet, unprepared to again face persuasion or death. Marak could wait. She needed Elyon.

Darsal went into a full gallop over the dunes, streaking over sand for almost a mile before remembering to circle back to catch up to the others.

She wasn't given the chance. Marak appeared out of nowhere and grabbed her horse by the reins. The animal squealed and reared. Darsal hit the ground hard. He jumped down after her and grabbed both arms. Darsal lashed at him, tried to get up, but Marak's grip held fast.

"What are you thinking? If you were going to run away, you should have done it long before now!"

"I wasn't running! I was watching for Eram's men. I used to be Guard. It's habit."

Marak tensed, searched her face, then exhaled and plopped beside her, one arm across her in a defensive posture.

"Dars—" He took a ragged breath. "Oh, Darsal, what did you go do that for?"

"I . . . wasn't thinking."

Without warning, Marak leaned over and held her against his chest. She was too stunned to react. "No, you weren't." The growl had left his voice.

He lifted her carefully and rocked her for a few moments

before letting her sit. Her mind reeled, desperate to catch up. Marak pushed back her headscarf and brushed away strands of hair that had fallen loose of her braids.

Elyon, is he . . . ?

"I'm sorry. You went into a gallop, and we all thought . . . Well, it was me go after you or my men."

He wiped her face with the edge of his cloak. Darsal caught his wrist and rose up on her knees, wincing at the pain in her ribs.

His expression went flat. He put her headscarf back up and drew it across her face. And she felt it. In the depth of her being was the cruel emotion she hadn't known from the time Billos had thrown his arms around her and saved them all, to the day Marak tried to kill her but turned his back forever on that door.

And now she knew it again, a thousand times stronger.

Marak had frozen. He shook his head at her, even though he looked just as stunned as she felt.

"It isn't possible, Darsal. It would never work."

"But you do care for me. Don't you?"

"We don't have feelings for albinos, Darsal. Nor do they for us."

"Forget us and them!" She knotted her fists and leaned toward him.

He cared. He had to.

His hands were on her arms, but not in the rough fashion she was accustomed to. Marak didn't quite make eye contact. When he looked away, her emotions boiled over.

"I like you, woman. I trust you. Isn't that enough?"

Darsal squeezed her eyes shut. The volcano was erupting, and she could do nothing about it, nothing about the pain in her heart and the forbidden words gnawing at the tip of her tongue.

"Marak, the truth is I . . . I love you. Don't you understand? I've stayed for you!"

"You can't!"

He hadn't moved. The man was like ice. He'd have to kill her now. He didn't have a choice, not after this. And that infuriated her.

"Why not? Who says I can't love you? You're human, right? Or is the truth that I'm not human enough for you? Is that it?"

"Darsal—"

"I love you, Marak, and I want you to love me, too, and see Elyon loves you, and drown with him and become like me!"

"Darsal."

"But if that doesn't happen, then I really am doing all this for nothing, and I really am a complete fool like you say! It's—"

Marak snatched her off balance, one arm around her. His lips brushed her neck, her scarred cheek. "I doubted."

Darsal looked up at his face. Marak tipped her head back and cupped the base of her chin in his warm fingers.

"General."

The greeting sliced between them. Marak threw her back. Darsal scrambled away, and they both found their feet. She yanked her cowl over her face, pulse spiking. Caught. Caught and dead.

Cassak sat on horseback before them. He dropped down and

threw the reins at Darsal. The general and the captain sized each other up.

Cassak saluted Marak, expression grim. "The Eramites have been following us."

Marak remained silent.

That cold sensation slithered along, the same she had felt from Sucrow before.

"I sent some messengers to remind them this was not a war party nor a band of spies. We do not wish a fight; we are at peace and intend to stay that way. It is only a temporary solution, however."

Darsal peeked up at her general. He traded another look with Cassak, then gave a nod, but it was a full minute before he spoke, choosing his words carefully.

"That will suffice. Peace is best for all at this stage. Tell them to keep their fires far from our expedition. We go only as far as the canyon."

Cassak looked at Darsal, staring until she could no longer stand it. "The road is muddy." His eyes drifted back to her general. "Perhaps we should heed the warning."

Marak looked angry. "What will you do?"

The captain hesitated. "I will watch. There is no need, as of yet, to report the matter to Qurong. I haven't decided what, if anything, to say to Sucrow."

Darsal's head shot up. They were not talking about the rebel general, the half-breed Eram. Cassak was warning Marak about falling in love with an albino.

"Some treasures are best left hidden." Marak bowed his head. "Thank you, Captain. I'll see you promoted."

Cassak frowned. "It would not be wise at this time." He came closer to Darsal and inspected her, grimaced at the smell of her skin.

The captain was making a pronouncement. Judgment on their sin.

Marak mounted Cassak's horse. His and Darsal's had run off. Cassak bound Darsal's wrists and tossed the other end of the chain to Marak.

Cassak leaned close to Darsal's ear and whispered. "Another stunt like that, and I *will* go to Qurong. After today it is over. Understood?"

Renounce her love and save Marak's life.

Darsal's heart sank to her heels. She couldn't let him go. Elyon had changed her heart for these Scabs, for Marak, and he wouldn't release her. So she couldn't release Marak.

Cassak released her and gave his horse a thump. "Good."

To Marak, Cassak said, "I'll find your horses. The canyon is just over that rise." He pointed. "Welcome to the Teardrop."

TWELVE

Marak towed Darsal up the rise. Cassak followed at a distance, then disappeared once more into the dunes. Of all the foolish things he could have done! He'd let his guard down for one moment. For one second tasted the forbidden.

At the same second Cassak came looking for his missing general.

"You executed your own family on principle," he could imagine the captain saying. "You round up albinos and kill them on orders, out of loyalty. And now you throw your principles out the window for what—a rotting corpse of a woman? Why don't you just make love to the dead!"

Maybe Cassak was right to steal the amulet and take it to the priest. Marak was getting too close to this. Either Sucrow had used his magic on Cassak, or Cassak really did throw loyalty and friendship to the wind. Which?

At the top of the rise, Marak stopped his horse and stared down over the teardrop-shaped gash in the desert floor. The north end made the bulge, the south the point.

As if Elyon himself were crying.

Now, that was a silly thought. As silly as taking an albino woman in his arms and kissing her. As silly as wishing he'd gone ahead and given in to the impulse completely.

Darsal stood near the horse's head, stroking its neck. The chain that now bound her to his horse clattered. "I've never seen one this big."

"Seen what? A canyon?" He furrowed his brow.

The canyon was barren from what he could see, save a narrow path that wandered around the rim before starting down. The rest of their number had already approached but hadn't started down.

"A Black Forest."

"Cassak's watching our backs. What are you worried about?" He started down, wondering if his old friend at his back still meant anything to him. Darsal submitted to the pull of her tether.

"I'm worried about what happens when Josef uses that medallion."

He paused and looked down at her. "Why are you always so insistent that you're in the right? This reasoning is what has Cassak trying to decide if he's going to inform Qurong as to what I've done."

She closed her mouth.

"That wasn't fair. You may take your own life lightly, Darsal, but why must you expect the same of me? Isn't it enough that I—"

He still couldn't say it, and hated the question that would follow.

Darsal's brow creased.

Forget it.

Marak spurred the horse fast enough to make Darsal run and unable to ask any more questions. Not enough to drag her.

Run Darsal did, easier than he'd expected.

Marak pressed on. Sucrow, Josef and Arya, his three commanders, and the two Throaters waited at the edge of the canyon, their eyes fixed on him and his rebellious albino slave. Marak slowed to a walk. He didn't look at her.

"I see you've caught her," Sucrow sneered, turning his staff. "That should remind you not to trust the wench."

"Who said I did?"

He glimpsed the rim of the canyon, splashed orange and red with sunlight. Purple and rust streaked along the upper portion. Stunning. A bridge spanned the length of the teardrop, and, just as Cassak said, a path led around the edge of the canyon and down into its basin.

He looked instead at Josef, whose appearance had changed. The younger man's skin was pale, almost transparent. His body looked harder, more muscular. Skin and hair almost aglow. And his eyes. A purple cast.

"Show us the way."

"We'll have to leave the horses partway down. The brush gets too thick toward the south end." Josef reached inside his shirt. "It's steep."

"There's more than brush down there." Darsal's voice carried a strange edge to it.

"No one asked your opinion," Sucrow snapped. Marak didn't take the time to correct him.

"Patience," Josef said. "She is correct. Yet such is why we possess the amulet. Withdraw such."

Marak eyed him, curious at the strange speech. He took the medallion out of his pocket.

A loud shriek crashed in from overhead, accompanied by a whoosh of leathery wings. Marak ducked, arm raised, and looked up.

His mind revolted against what his eyes saw. Shadows fell over their faces, as if there had been an eclipse. A black, furry bat the size of a human child with beady, red eyes flew at them again, claws extended, fangs bared.

The entire expedition fell into shock.

Josef snatched the amulet from Marak, held up his hand, and shouted. The beast dove over their heads, circled high, and swooped down into the canyon.

The bat disappeared into a black gash in the ground. Trees with black bark and wood sprang out of the canyon several hundred feet and blotted out the sun. The muddy road ran around the edge of the canyon before heading straight down, beneath the bridge, completely lost to the cold woods.

He heard Sucrow unleash a tirade at him for stealing the amulet back.

"Now do you believe me?" Josef and Darsal spoke at once, then silenced when they realized it. "The amulet shall protect us from such," Josef finished.

Believe them? Marak's heart lodged in his throat. Josef's eyes hardened. Alien, inhuman.

There was a black forest. *Darsal was right. She was right all along.* A chill wound around his spine. *What else is she right about?*

He shook it off and rode high in the saddle, offered a hand to Darsal. "Get up." She obeyed without hesitation, content to lean against his back.

Boneheaded fool . . . Marak could almost see his brother's narrowed eyes, his crossed arms, his exasperation.

Not now. You mean not ever. And didn't you make a promise to Darsal? He'd forgotten. It was insignificant. But Darsal was right; he never should have let Sucrow take the girl.

That's more like it.

Would you get out of my head?

I'm dead, brother.

Marak grunted, then turned his attention to the priest. "Sucrow, release Arya. Arya, ride with Josef, and the two of you take us down."

"But she—"

"I said let her go!" Marak snapped.

A Shataiki had just attacked them and vanished into its lair. They were walking into hell. And the priest was still on his quest for power.

Sucrow untied Arya and allowed her to swing off the horse. Arya marched over to Josef and jumped up behind him. The priest growled and remounted. Marak ordered his commanders and the two Throaters to wait for them to return.

He gave Josef the word, and the three horses started down.

Josef took them around to a ledge with more slope to it and picked his way toward the creek. The lower they descended, the darker the forest became. Bat wings slapped around them, and the occasional pair of beady eyes glared through the trees. Sucrow began to chant softly, in words Marak didn't understand.

Darsal slid her arm around his waist.

He took her hand and, in the darkness that now surrounded them all, kissed it lightly.

THIRTEEN

Johnis led them downward in a spiral trajectory, like going down a drain or a whirlpool. Ever downward, into a pit. Into sewage and waste. Pitch-black trees with rotten, black leaves that curled. Even the grass and dirt were black. The canyon was perilous, and everything was obscenely still.

Deeper they went, the droplet shape narrowing with time, walls caving in around them. Darsal heard a dripping somewhere. A black waterfall.

"Elyon, save us," she whispered.

A bat screeched overhead, underscoring her plea.

"Were you ever really alone, Darsal? Really?" Elyon asked gently.

I'm alone now.

But that wasn't true either.

Marak was here. Johnis and Silvie were alive. The rest of the Circle was alive somewhere.

As long as Johnis's plan didn't play out, they would stay that way. And right now she had no means of stopping him.

Except Elyon's charge of love.

Would that be enough . . . ?

The forest taunted her. It closed in around her and groped at her, crushed her lungs. Sucrow was chanting somewhere, an incantation that sounded familiar to her, though she couldn't remember where she'd heard such a hideous thing.

Thoughts of the last lair she'd crawled into clawed at her, mocked her.

They reached the bottom and followed a murky, stale stream until the path narrowed too much for the horses. Darsal didn't want to leave the animals, but Marak had her tether all three, and they pressed on.

"You're sure you know where you're going?" she asked Johnis.

"I'm sure, albino," he snapped.

"There are things stronger than amulets," Darsal whispered back, ignoring his jibe. "Stronger than Leedhan and bats."

Johnis didn't respond. He led them on foot through thorny brush and thick, black mud, traveling along a streambed. Even Sucrow held his silence. All remained pensive and still. The stream rushed into a waterfall, and Johnis led them around the dark, bubbling water.

A shaman once had told Darsal that bodies of water were living things. They laughed and played along the shore. This water was different though. This water cackled like a villain about to take his prey as it spilled over a hillside and splashed into a cauldron below.

A shallow clearing opened up, creating a kind of bowl. Headstones rose up out of the water, wrapped in mist. In the middle of the small lake was a platform.

An eerie, purplish haze enveloped them. Darsal pressed against Marak, then remembered Cassak's warning and shifted away. All around them the trees were weighed down by black bats with glowing red eyes and sharp claws and teeth.

Memories haunted her mind. She had to work to push them aside.

Johnis looked at Silvie, then Sucrow. "I need some water. And the rest. You've brought it?"

Sucrow nodded. He withdrew from his bag a silver bowl that Silvie took from him. She waded into the water. Next came a clay bowl and a small leather pouch. The priest began to chant.

Johnis took a silver knife from Sucrow; then they both followed Silvie out to the platform, their supplies held over their heads.

Darsal and Marak waited on the bank. Johnis couldn't hear her. Darsal sank into a crouch and put her chin on her fists, elbows on her knees.

Bloody Leedhan.

Johnis stood sentinel, his face white, while Sucrow and Silvie made preparations. Silvie filled the silver bowl with water and placed it in the center. Sucrow took what looked like a makeshift altar and set it out. Incense soon wafted through the air and flooded their nostrils.

A nauseating stench. Where had she smelled that? The priest's invocation continued, witnessed by hundreds of red-eyed Shataiki with visions of carnage in their heads.

What was Johnis doing? It was supposed to be a simple incantation.

Darsal could barely watch. So Johnis had needed Sucrow after all. Sucrow withdrew a bird with bound wings from a small cage she hadn't seen earlier and killed it, pouring its blood over the altar. The bats swarming around them began to thrum.

Johnis placed the medallion around his neck in open view and waited for a signal from Sucrow. By his expression, something like terror had overtaken him, but was it his or the Leedhan's?

Silvie took the knife from Sucrow. She would never relinquish it, Darsal knew. The slender, lithe woman looked more serpentine than ever and kept eying Sucrow as if judging the distance for a successful death throw.

Sucrow stopped chanting. He held aloft something silver and round in his right hand for the bats to see.

Johnis found his confidence and stood to one side of the altar. He puffed out his chest, raised his chin high, and spoke clipped words in a language Darsal didn't recognize. He reached into his robe and withdrew a yellow, rotted, maggoty fruit that was bigger than his palm and held it at arm's length in both hands.

The bats fell quiet.

"I come seeking audience with your guardian!" Johnis demanded of the Shataiki. "I come with a gift, should he desire such! Or is Derias a coward?"

Dissention and arguing rustled through the ranks.

A Shataiki twice the size of the others flapped overhead, circled, and swooped down onto the platform, landing directly across from Johnis before the altar, his wings partly folded.

"Who comes to my home?" the beast asked. His eyes didn't leave the fruit. He ran his long, pink tongue over his black lips and sneered. "So you survived. And returned."

Johnis raised his chin. He started to change. To turn completely transparent. His eyes took on the purple gaze. Lips curled into a wicked sneer. Animallike.

The Leedhan.

Even Silvie looked unnerved by his behavior. Derias made a coughing sound that was probably a laugh. His eyes narrowed and brightened. "Then you understand the danger."

"I concern myself not with such risks." Johnis tightened his jaw. "I present to you a means of restoring that which has so long been denied you. The glory of the sons of our Great One, our lord Teeleh, shall at last be made complete again. These trappings which now bind you shall no longer hinder. What say you, mighty guardian?"

Johnis would know better. The entity had to be lying. Shataiki could never regain "glory," assuming they'd ever had any.

The bat drooled over the fruit. He wanted it, badly, but something was holding him back. Only one choice would allow them to find out. Was it base to ask Elyon to bestow wisdom upon a Shataiki?

"You think me so easily swayed?" Derias stroked his chin with a claw. His gaze flicked from the fruit to the sacrificed bird to Johnis. "Begone!"

"We have an agreement." Johnis's voice was husky. Seductive.

"I am not persuaded."

"Such is for you and you alone, my prince. Taste and see." Johnis opened his free hand toward Silvie. She passed him the knife. He cut the fruit open, returned the knife to her, and smelled half of the fruit.

Darsal's stomach churned.

Johnis said something so soft she couldn't even hear his voice. She only saw his mouth move.

But the bat heard. Silence lingered.

Then Derias turned to Sucrow and took the bird from his outstretched hand. Johnis watched, blank faced, while the Shataiki tore its prey to pieces and fed. Darsal imagined Johnis was the bird, his soul ripped apart by cruel talons.

Silvie whispered to Johnis, and the bat replied.

"Such is not within reach forever," Johnis warned.

The throng of Shataiki fluttered in the trees. Darsal grabbed for one of Marak's knives. He pulled her hand away.

"Take and eat, most excellent of beasts." Johnis offered the fruit to the bat one last time, his words lost in the air that clung to them.

No, Johnis, no.

Derias shrieked and took off into the air, circled high beyond the trees, and dove back down, wings folded, straight for Johnis.

Darsal grabbed Marak's knife and whipped her arm back to throw. Marak grabbed her, pinned her down, and took the knife away.

The bat let out another roar and whooshed past Johnis's head, knocking him down. His talons closed around the fruit, and he swerved upward again. The other Shataiki took flight, and hundreds upon hundreds joined their queen in the sky. They screeched and dove over the humans' heads.

Marak threw himself over Darsal.

"Did he eat it?" Darsal screamed. "Did he eat it?"

"I don't know!"

Darsal fought at first, then remembered the general wasn't going to hurt her. He scooped her up and ran with her in a dark, hot cocoon.

"Josef!" Marak yelled. "Get down from the—"

Johnis shouted over the din. Water splashed when he jumped in and started swimming.

"What's happening?" Darsal demanded. "What's going on? Did they take it?"

"Yes," Marak snarled. "They're following us out. Josef ordered them to meet us in the sky but not to attack."

"Then put me down!"

"They aren't all obeying the command! I don't want you to—"

He grunted and fell flat on his face on top of her. He fought off the Shataiki clawing them. Another bat assaulted the first, and the pair rolled away. Marak picked Darsal back up and continued his retreat.

"Sucrow! Forget that! Come on!"

"Marak!" She threw her arms around his neck.

"Hold on!" He lost his footing, and they both went flying.

Darsal fell, her head smashing against rock, with Marak's weight slamming into her. Red and yellow stars, then darkness.

FOURTEEN

Johnis raced with the others back through the forest, with two million Shataiki at their heels. Shaeda dug into him, riding him like a horse to steer clear of the bats. Derias had relayed the order not to attack the humans, but the ranks were unstable, and the beasts kept breaking the line to harass them. The queen had taken the bait.

And he was enraged.

The bats roared around them, their wings like thunderclaps, darkening the sky further. Silvie scrambled ahead of Johnis and the others and went for the horses. She yelled.

Shaeda's power surged through him, charging his muscles and shoving blood through his body with enough force to mow down a Horde army.

Johnis and Marak, still carrying Darsal, were only seconds

behind. Sucrow straggled. Johnis tripped over something solid and fumbled. He rolled sideways and jumped back up, looked down.

A horse's leg bone. Grimacing, Johnis darted around the corpse. All three horses were completely torn to shreds and stripped of flesh.

Marak's knife was in his hand. He shifted his wriggling bundle over one shoulder. Disgusting, Johnis thought, holding an albino like that.

"They did this?"

"Better the horses than us. Can't she walk?"

With a snarl, Marak started back up the path, seething over the dead horses. Johnis hurried after him with Silvie and Sucrow.

On and on they fled, breathless and fumbling in the unnatural night. Shaeda made Johnis swift and surefooted, skirting up the sides of the rock faces and canyon with ease. Twice the general stumbled with his burden, and twice Johnis caught him and helped him regain his footing.

"Just leave her!" Johnis said the second time. They were halfway up, and the wench was only slowing them down. "Leave her already! How do you stand the smell of the worm?"

Marak glowered at him. "She'll die at the appointed time!"

"So now you favor the albino," Johnis snapped, appalled at the thought. Shaeda bared her teeth in scorn. "Will you be joining Eram's ranks?"

Marak struck him with his free hand. "Mind your tongue, boy. Bats or no, I'll have your head and—"

"You think you can destroy me?" Johnis rose from the ground. Shaeda bristled, terrified of the Shataiki and ready to engage any lesser being. This general was now simply a nuisance. Johnis's hands curled like talons.

Marak turned his back. "You can kill her with the others."

He marched on, heedless of the rest. Johnis started after him, compelled to tear the general's heart out and feed it to Derias.

Silvie grasped his shoulder. Shaeda tensed. "Enough," Silvie said. "Deal with the albinos first. Then the general."

FIFTEEN

Darsal regained consciousness while she was still slung over the general's shoulder. She grunted as her teeth snapped together, chin bouncing off Marak. He took the final steps up the side of the canyon and set Darsal on her own two feet. With Shataiki still swarming in the cauldron, they hadn't dared slow. Her head throbbed where she'd hit it. Blood caked the back of her neck.

The blow she'd taken seemed to jar her general more than anything else.

"Can you walk?" He had an edge to his voice. Who knew it would take a swarm of blood-lusty Shataiki to unnerve a general?

Darsal staggered, wincing. "Of course I can walk."

Her general's gaze lingered on her.

His touch was astonishingly light. Those big hands that could crush held her steady with all the care one would give a newborn.

His eyes were wild from the chase, lit with terror at the implications of the carnage these beasts could create.

The Throaters were quiet, faces ashen and set like flint in an attempt to conceal their obvious fear. Good. Nothing like a trip to hell to put the fear of Elyon in a cutthroat.

Sucrow stood gaping, awestruck by the sight of his master's servants. The Dark Priest fell to his knees and uttered a prayer to his god, thanking him for their success thus far. Darsal frowned.

"I'll be surprised if he doesn't sacrifice to Teeleh," she scoffed.

Johnis had won this round. Assuming any deal made with a Shataiki could be considered a win. Johnis had the power and the medallion that controlled the bats. And Marak's ear.

"She is using him, daughter."

She bristled at that. *What will she do?*

Elyon's silence made her skin crawl.

Desert greeted them. Stark, silent desert that vanished beneath a shadowy, writhing curtain. Marak ordered the torches lit. The bats howled and shrieked, keeping their distance from the flames.

"We have four days," Johnis warned Marak in that deep, husky voice that had to belong to the entity Gabil spoke of. "We've no time to waste. You've brought fresh horses as instructed?"

In answer, horses and riders pounded toward them, kicking up a dust storm. From out of the sands came Cassak and some of his men, leading horses. Ignoring the surprise of the rest of the group, Cassak brought a stallion to Marak and Darsal.

Captain and general traded long, cold looks. What had become of these two, once friends?

Without a word, Marak helped Darsal astride, then leaped behind her.

Shataiki filled the canyon and poured out of it into the sky, a giant black tornado, a whirlwind of leather, fur, fangs, and claws mottled with red, beady eyes.

Johnis, Silvie, and Sucrow mounted their new horses. Johnis held his accursed medallion in one hand and looked to the blackened sky, enthralled, terrified, his eyes stained purple. He was speaking in the foreign language again.

Johnis afraid of the Shataiki?

No, the thing inside of him was.

At this moment Darsal feared him more than Sucrow. Johnis knew no boundaries beyond the thoughts of his heart. Right now he either wasn't listening to his heart or his heart had turned as black as the hurricane gathering above them.

"Are you ready?" Marak whispered into her shoulder.

Had it really only been a few days since Johnis asked her the same question?

"I'm ready to die, Marak. But this? Never. This is mindless slaughter." Darsal straightened in the saddle. The acid ball in her stomach knotted further at her epiphany.

Johnis was still reciting whatever wicked spell pleased him as Sucrow lifted his clawlike hands to the sky. Silvie pricked her finger with the silver ceremonial dagger, for reasons Darsal didn't know. But then, the girl seemed to have developed a fetish for those knives. Cassak kept a baleful watch, ordering his men not to panic, to keep the line.

None of them had ever seen so much as one Shataiki—much less this swarm of two million.

Derias, the Shataiki queen, erupted from the throng of beasts and circled Johnis, shrieking over his head. He spiraled back into the cloud, roaring against his entrapment. His long, cold shadow eased by.

"Have you heard of the mountain called Ba'al Bek?" Johnis asked, his voice still the strange sound of one possessed by a Leedhan.

Ba'al Bek. Darsal's eyes narrowed. Why did that sound familiar? Certainly she hadn't learned it from this earth.

"No." Marak tensed. The certainty in his voice had dissipated. Sucrow was not the only one capable of sorcery.

The Leedhan . . .

"I will show you the way. We have four days to reach it. But first we require the blood of the ruler of this world."

Marak's eyes narrowed. "Qurong's blood."

Johnis gave a sharp nod. "Only a little."

"Why?"

Marak glared at Johnis. Darsal watched him. Her general's eyes fixed onto Johnis's purplish-blue ones and seemed half-drugged. Johnis's mouth curled into a wicked, coy grin.

"I must perform a ceremony preceding the incantation," Sucrow said. "It can only be done at Ba'al Bek."

The general didn't seem to notice. He was seeing something else entirely.

"General Marak." Darsal cleared her throat, unwilling to touch him in front of the priest. The trance broke.

"You know where this place is?" Marak snapped at Sucrow and Johnis.

"We must make haste," Johnis said in Shaeda's voice. "Such is two days beyond Middle, and a day and a half must pass before we reach the esteemed leader."

SIXTEEN

The eclipsing clouds of Shataiki merged together, blotting out the sun entirely. No moon, no stars, nothing but millions of red dots marking the beasts' faces. Their unblinking eyes stared down at the band of humans below. Overhead the Shataiki queen raged and thrashed, darting in and out of the throng, barely restrained. Derias snarled and howled against his imprisonment.

The hours passed, and evening came, further pitching the blackness. The cold night air strangled Darsal. How the others still knew where they were going, she had no idea. They were lost out here. At the mercy of savage monsters.

Her unease returned. Marak's outbursts of affection had ebbed. Another half hour passed. She couldn't abide both his silence and the Shataiki's wrath.

"Tell me about Jordan," she said. His mind had refused to

make the connection between his family and the albinos, between not serving Elyon and serving Teeleh. Maybe in drawing the two brothers together she could make him see . . .

The general didn't respond for a minute. Then he clicked his tongue at the horse and rode forward, a short distance away from the others. Away from Sucrow.

"He was my brother."

Stubborn Scab. "And . . . ?"

"He'd be a captain by now if the disease hadn't taken him." The general looked ahead, his voice quiet. For a minute he looked like his brother, hidden beneath a shell.

"I wish I'd known him better."

"Me too." A half smile crossed Marak's face. "Stubborn fool."

THE EXPEDITION PARTY RODE ON TO THE STEADY THRUM OF rushing bat wings, punctuated by Derias's snarls. Johnis, Silvie, and Sucrow argued occasionally, but even they were mostly silent. Silvie wouldn't relinquish Sucrow's dagger. The priest, understandably, wanted it back.

"What was it like?" Marak's voice rumbled through Darsal's bones and roused her. She sat up straighter and looked around. He'd ridden out again, separating them from prying ears.

"Drowning. I never asked Jordan. You told me how it happened. But . . . there's always more with you."

She summoned the memory back. "Terrifying. Exhilarating.

The water's cold as ice. And deep, impossibly deep. The deeper you go, the warmer the water becomes. Darker. And soon you realize Elyon's in the water with you."

She went on, explaining how her lungs burned and how, finally, she'd breathed in the water. Like a fish.

The general listened, emotionless. "Was Jordan out of his mind?" he breathed.

Darsal kept her voice even before speaking of his family's deaths. That wound was still ragged and festering, hot with blood. "Were you out of your mind when you tried to save them and stay loyal to Qurong? You didn't have to do that, Marak. Elyon knows it'd have been easier if you hadn't."

For a full minute they merely stared at each other. Marak was listening now. And he was so close she could feel his body heat. But in five minutes he might consider killing her again.

Her jaw set. Idly, she fingered Jordan's pendant, but she didn't notice until she saw the general staring at it.

"I'm not afraid for myself, Marak." She didn't look. Didn't want to see his reaction to that. He could take it however he liked.

Elyon . . .

Seconds ticked by.

"People die whether albino or not, Darsal."

She drew a breath. "Then I have already failed."

TORCHLIGHT DID LITTLE MORE THAN ILLUMINATE THEIR faces in this unnatural darkness. Cassak spoke from horseback to his four scouts, who were flanked by servants carrying the flames. Sucrow was right—Marak no longer considered him a friend, not since Jordan and Rona's arrests. He hadn't seen it before, but now, with the growing rift following their executions, he could see plainly.

And now Marak was falling for an albino. Worse, Marak knew Cassak had stolen the amulet right from under his nose and taken it to the priest. He'd taken the copies of the journals, too, but thus far the general hadn't noticed. More of the priest's skills.

"Keep the torches in rotation," he said to the scouts. "And relay from beyond the cloud. Try not to agitate the beasts." Cassak glimpsed the priest riding up. "You're dismissed."

He narrowed his eyes at Sucrow's approach, staff in hand. He still detested the priest and his cutthroats, and he had no intention of watching Marak send himself down a hole. Maybe this would wake him up and snap him back into the real world, where albinos were the enemy to be destroyed, and loyalty to Qurong was to be held above all else.

Loyalty, integrity, honor. Where were Marak's in all of this?

"What do you want now?" Cassak snapped. That strange sensation swept over him again, the numbing one that left him dizzy and wondering what he'd just done.

"Patience," Sucrow answered. Cassak circled him, both irritated and unable to simply leave. He had to do this, had to make Marak see the truth.

"Do you have the copies?"

The war journal. Marak had made a copy and put it in his

captain's care shortly after discovering it. Upon learning their former general's information, the Desecration hadn't taken long to concoct. Cassak had helped develop it.

He nodded and gave Sucrow the book, along with his report on Jordan's death. "Don't expect anything else."

Dark humor crossed the priest's face. "Of course not, Captain." His staff turned in his hand. Cassak's throat tickled, making him cough.

"You're still prepared for the other, are you not?"

Josef and Arya. Sucrow wanted Josef and Arya dead, the entity gone. Why, Cassak could only speculate, but there were reasonable explanations.

"Now it is you who requires patience," Cassak warned. "The men will be ready. But beyond that I wash my hands of this."

Sucrow chuckled. His hand moved in a circular motion.

Cassak scratched his neck.

"Still believe yourself loyal to the general, do you?"

"That is not your concern." Or was it? Lately the priest was making more sense than the general, though Cassak hardly dared admit it.

"Well, understand this then, Captain: the general's loyalties no longer lie with Qurong. I suggest you make up your mind."

SEVENTEEN

Time was running out to get back to Qurong and on to Ba'al Bek, wherever that was. As far as Darsal could tell, only the Leedhan actually knew.

Darsal couldn't stand the sight of those beady, red eyes staring at her from all sides any longer. Skirmishes among the bats disrupted the stillness, but all was otherwise well. In a matter of hours, she would be dead. She had not won Marak. She had not stopped Johnis.

Ill at ease, she shifted in the saddle. This place was full of devilry.

The Shataiki ranks began to rustle, the throngs shifting into formation. They were hungry, Johnis had said, ravenous for a kill, their nostrils riddled with the scent of their favored prey.

Marak grated his teeth, irritated at being pulled in two directions.

"Josef, one bat gets out of hand and I'll have your head. I'll keep the head and give the body to the bats. Understood?"

Johnis didn't answer right away; instead he looked up at the swarm he controlled. "Understood."

They were exhausted but pressed on into the night. Soon all was quiet. Not one wing fluttered. Darsal heard nothing except the blood surging through her veins and her throbbing, pulsing heart.

As one, the Shataiki surrounding them roared and took flight. Screams shook the night. Darsal jumped and strained to see, but all was black. Then the shrieks were overpowered by the sound of Shataiki feeding on flesh. Living or dead, she did not know.

The expedition party fell into a panic. The Scabs rushed around, trying to find the source of the slaughter, shouting in the midst of Shataiki whipping about them. The bats clawed and bit, wings open wide.

Darsal leaped from the saddle and ran, searching for a weapon. A bat caught her by the shoulders and ripped into her back with its claws. She screeched and kicked it in the gut, refusing to fall to a beast almost as big as she was. It knocked her down.

She grabbed a rock and smashed it into the head of one. She glimpsed a green eye among the red but didn't have time to respond. Two now fell on her, fighting over her body. One had her by the leg, another by the wrist. They ripped at her flesh and clung to her. Blood seeped from her wounds. She smashed a claw into the hard-packed sand.

Bloodlust sent the rest of the bats into a frenzy. The entire mass began to swarm and rage, boiling in a kind of cauldron.

Metal rang out and slashed through the meat of one of the bats on top of her with a sick, sucking sound. The beast roared as it died. The second turned on her rescuer and left her in the dust. Darsal rolled away and jumped to all fours, still in search of a weapon. The Scabs were fighting now, torches lit and swords in hand. Johnis and Silvie were in there . . . somewhere . . . shouting to one another.

A powerful arm snatched her around the waist and ran, fighting Shataiki with one arm. Darsal was pinned against his side, dangling like a toy and being further battered by the melee.

Gruff utterances against the fates. Marak. The general dumped her on her feet as he barked another order. Darsal snatched a knife from his thigh sheath as he passed her and went back to back with him. Minutes passed. Minutes filled with the sounds of men and Shataiki in battle.

Then it was over.

All was pensive and riddled with nervous, quivering bodies. Darsal turned, eyes drawn to the commotion behind her. The warriors and Throaters had formed a circle around Marak. Torchlight cast odd shadows over their faces. Her eyes followed their gaze until she saw Marak. He stood holding Johnis by his throat, his feet dangling above the ground. Johnis's arms were wrapped around Marak's wrist, his face twisted in pain. A standoff.

Cassak held Silvie by the arms, restraining her. But why did Marak have Johnis?

Johnis's skin and eyes took on their recent unnatural look. His face twisted into a hard snarl. "Release me," he warned.

"You ordered them to attack," Marak growled. He flung Johnis down, realized Darsal had his knife, and swiped it back. The weapon sang into its sheath.

Johnis landed in a crouch. Wild-eyed. "You doubt me?" His voice had turned low and inhuman. Shaeda.

Had she persuaded him to set the Shataiki on them? If so, why? Or had they come after Shaeda?

Marak's sword ran red, dripping on the ground. Now he raised the weapon. "Is this the best the great Josef has to offer?"

Johnis still looked possessed. As though he might spring at Marak and slit his throat without hesitation. "Your men interfered with their hunt."

The anger radiated off Marak's body.

"She is lying." Darsal heard Gabil and glanced around. The Roush's wing vanished behind a rock. She tensed. If the amulet could reveal the Shataiki, it could reveal a Roush.

"I did not break our agreement," Johnis insisted.

The general's sword came to rest at Johnis's throat. "Do you prefer to die kneeling or standing?"

Silvie grumbled from behind Johnis. He turned to look at her, and the two traded a look Darsal didn't understand.

The look Cassak gave Marak, though, was clear. One wrong move now, one mistake, and the captain's hand would be forced. Cassak would declare Marak a traitor. Marak would die.

But Marak had also given his word, and he would not break it.

Would she lose both Marak and Johnis in one foolish moment?

"I prefer not to die at all." Johnis sneered and fingered his medallion. His eyes—Shaeda's eyes—were ruthless.

If Shaeda attacked . . .

Lose Marak or Johnis or both.

"Wait, General!" All eyes fell on Darsal. "This was a mistake." She stepped up beside him, then between Johnis and Marak. "General, don't kill him. This was . . . an accident."

Marak turned, obviously angry. "An accident?"

"A Shataiki thought I was attacking Josef. It wouldn't do for their master to perish."

Darsal waited. He wouldn't buy it. Marak would know this was all an act. That she was lying. And she knew it was absurd to claim the bats were protecting Johnis from an alleged attack by a desperate albino. But the Scabs might not know that. Not even Sucrow had seen this before. And Johnis didn't want to die.

"General," Cassak said finally. "We need your decision."

Marak looked at Johnis. "Is this true?"

Hesitation. Was Shaeda considering making him do something foolish?

Johnis regained control of himself. "Yes."

Marak sheathed his weapon and stormed off into the desert.

"The next to cause an *accident* dies."

EIGHTEEN

Darsal rode with Marak, lying still so he would think her asleep. So close to dawn, and yet the eclipse blacked out the sky. They rode ahead, with Sucrow somewhere behind, reciting a chant that sounded eerily familiar. Johnis and Silvie had also dropped back, whispering about something.

"Let it alone, Cassak. It was nothing." Marak's voice startled her. She shifted in the saddle. "She has her uses. I would like to keep her as long as is reasonable."

"Be fair. I'm not a fool." Cassak was impatient, his tone irreverent toward his general. But they were friends, which alone explained his casual behavior.

"You don't intend to execute her at all."

Unfortunately Cassak was more observant than the others.

"She'll die soon enough." Marak was still bristling. The edge in his voice was unmistakable.

"She should already be dead."

Marak grumbled something under his breath.

"So now you're doing her favors?" Cassak sounded scandalized. Why was he so bent on her being dead? He'd been patient enough with Marak's family. She dared a peek. Once more she saw the strange, starry-eyed serpent on the captain's throat.

What did it mean?

"I'm doing myself a favor."

"Jordan and Rona."

Another low, angry remark from the general. The silence lingered.

If pushed, what would Marak do?

A white wing caught her attention. Gabil, hiding in the shadows. His green eyes shone in the dark, then vanished. "Pay attention," she heard him whisper.

So this was about more than killing one lone albino. Everything came back to the Circle. To Thomas. To Elyon. She'd distracted herself from that truth. Hopefully not to the point of no return.

"Aren't you the one who said, 'Loyalty comes before and above all else'?" the captain was asking. Something was in his tone, a strained sound.

"Cassak . . ."

"Loyalty. Integrity. Honor. Those are the first things you taught me, and you learned everything from Martyn himself."

"I'm not betraying you, Cassak."

"I can't keep quiet forever." The two men fell silent. The unease was catching. It spread like poison. "She's like Rona." The captain paused. "Isn't she?"

Marak didn't answer.

"You need to execute her, Marak." Worry spilled into Cassak's voice. Worry or fear? Darsal leaned in. No, something was wrong. Cassak was acting. She wasn't entirely sure how she knew, but Cassak was no longer Cassak.

"You need to do it tonight. Don't throw away your career and your life for an albino wench."

"Don't call her that!"

"Why not? She *is*!"

"Because I—" Marak caught himself.

"You what?" the captain demanded. He snorted. "I don't believe this. You love an albino."

"I do not—"

"She's using you, Marak. Can't you see that?"

"There's nothing to see."

"I'm sorry, General." That part Darsal wanted to believe. Cassak's voice was strained, conflicted. "I can't protect you this time." He rode away.

Darsal waited until Cassak was gone before shifting. Marak rode farther ahead.

"We have no time. It's over, Darsal. Cassak will have me marked a traitor shortly after the business with the Circle is done."

Darsal let that sink in and didn't like the implications. She wanted so much more and knew it would never happen. Marak was resolute.

Adrenaline pounded through her, making her dizzy. His hand lingered a second before releasing her, always too soon.

Darsal grabbed the reins. "Come on."

"Middle is the other—"

"We need water, Marak. We need to—"

He went rigid and spun her toward him. "I've been far too lenient if you truly think that after so little time I would be swayed."

He knew she wanted him to drown. Of course he did.

"I save your life and you ask me to kill myself?" He let go of her. "Isn't my love enough?"

A flash of heat made its way up Darsal's spine. She forced herself to inhale, forced her mind to catch up. He still didn't understand.

"Love is deeper than this, Marak. So much—"

"I spared your friends at your request. I let you lie for them. I spared your life when I should have sentenced you on the spot. All of this, Darsal, and still you want my life?"

"I gave you mine." Darsal breathed deep. "That wasn't fair." She backed down, trying to reclaim whatever was left of this mad relationship. With Elyon's gentle prompting as her guide, she softened.

"You love Elyon, don't you, Marak?"

He didn't answer.

No, he wouldn't admit that much. But just maybe . . .

"Don't do it for me. Do it for Elyon. Don't you wonder where he went? Why he's silent? Haven't you wondered why all of these things are happening and still Elyon says nothing?"

Marak let out a low, raspy breath, irritated because he didn't want to answer.

"Do you really believe I came from another world, Marak? That I did not bathe for ten years?"

"I believe you. But what does that have to do with—"

"Jordan watched my skin turn in the dungeon, my general. They watched me rot in a cell for three days before Jordan helped me escape. I didn't believe him either."

That stopped him.

"I didn't believe him until the water went into my lungs and I stopped breathing air and started breathing water. I just wanted Elyon more than I wanted to live."

"Patience, daughter, patience," she heard Elyon chastise.

Marak thrust a finger in her face. "I am not having this conversation again. There will be no more talk of drowning."

"Marak—"

"No more, Darsal. No more."

NINETEEN

"You're sure you control the bats?" Silvie argued. She glared at him, commanding his attention with her voice. They rode a little ahead of the others, alone able to see inside this throng of shadows.

"Yes," Johnis snapped. He didn't mean to, but everything was purple haze, and Shaeda was anxious, so anxious. "She's terrified," he managed. "She's half-human; she can't fight this many . . ."

Shaeda tore into his thoughts. Blue and purple sparked across his mind, raking over his eyes. She didn't like him exposing her weaknesses, and the weakness was that she was only half-Shataiki. Powerful but mortal.

Her alluring gaze, her siren song . . .

Everything in him screamed to gallop ahead to Middle and get out from beneath this swarm of Shataiki, to lead the guardian queen where he willed, to silence that horrific sound of Derias lusty for a kill.

"Josef," Silvie said. His mind shifted, focusing on her. Shadows drifted over him, Shaeda's night vision retreating with her thoughts. "Why did the bats attack?"

"Because . . ."

The overpowering foresight took hold. He saw red desert fanning before him, giving way to canyons and a glorious mountain range full of desert trees and shrubs. The treacherous peaks were all angles and drop-offs, narrow cliffs and passes.

Beyond that, more desert, the land growing increasingly desolate. Jackals fought over dried bones, and carrion birds sought elsewhere for food, preying instead on the packs of hounds that fed off each other.

"Forget not, my pet . . . The human of my choosing was you. Yet such can alter . . . alter at a moment's breath . . ."

He smelled sulfur and felt as if his face were basking in the steam of hot springs, soothing his skin of the flaking, rotting cracks and the stiffening pain that overwhelmed him.

Twice divinely forsaken, by both Elyon and Teeleh, and thrice by the sons of men. And yet over the rise, beyond the cliffs, down the sharp ravine where craggy rocks grew from the earth like teeth, were the springs, near the mighty rushing river which the great tree spanned. A red river no human dared cross, for none could survive its falls. This river girded the earth as a belt and guarded the world of purebloods from the world of half-breeds.

From the far side of the world was no return . . .

How did you cross, then?

"Johnis!" Silvie dared use his real name. The vision retreated. He looked at her. "Why did the Shataiki attack us?"

Understanding washed over him. Shaeda looked upon her and raised his chin. "Take comfort, little female . . . Such will not occur again."

Silvie scowled. "Shaeda. It was you they wanted."

The Leedhan's thoughts darkened. Johnis's night vision returned. His gaze fell ahead. He kicked the horse and broke into a gallop, desperate for Middle, for home. Visions of blue forests and sweet, tangy badaiis swept over him.

He barely heard the general call after him. Let them keep pace.

TWENTY

The expedition party marched down the main road of Middle toward Qurong's white palace, now eclipsed by the shadow of Shataiki.

People ran out of their homes in panic, but Marak's men were ready. He rode at the head of the procession with Sucrow on his left. At his right, Cassak and Reyan. Warryn and the Throaters rode at Sucrow's far side.

Next came Johnis and Silvie. Behind them were the servants. Cassak had split his men to form a rear guard and two flanks to keep the streets clear of spectators.

Bats screeched and flapped, soaring through the city. Horns sounded the return of the priest and the general, announcing to all of Middle their success and the prize they brought Qurong.

The sun was already settling into the western sky, and they still hadn't acquired Qurong's blood for the ritual.

Johnis and Shaeda mentally rehearsed their plans. And very carefully, Johnis considered his personal interpretations of her instructions—interpretations that allowed him to manipulate her words so he could undermine her wishes on technicalities.

Only with Silvie did he have an opportunity for success. He could throw Shaeda off, but he couldn't plan anything without her knowing, could he?

"Do you remember what we talked about?" Johnis asked Silvie. Silvie had to do the bulk of the work; otherwise they would be discovered. He couldn't guard his thoughts from the entity inside him.

"Tread lightly, my Chosen One," Shaeda warned.

Silvie watched him, an eyebrow quirked. She pursed her lips. "I'll handle the priest," she said. "You watch the general."

Shaeda wanted to control the pair, not destroy them. But if controlling them meant they were dead, far easier. A permanent control.

Johnis sneered. Yes, as soon as he used the amulet, he would call on the Shataiki to circle. But what constituted a circle, anyway? Technicalities.

Shaeda came over him, heightening his perceptions. Silvie's eyes narrowed. Had the Leedhan heard him?

"We'll deal with the other later," Silvie scoffed. Her voice briefly cleared his head.

"Your attentions, my pet . . ."

They dismounted at the broad, white steps and came up the stairs. First Marak and Sucrow, then Johnis and Silvie. Darsal passed Johnis and came alongside Marak's flank. Warryn, Cassak, and Reyan followed, swords ready.

As they passed through the atrium to be admitted into Qurong's throne room, Johnis's hand brushed a leather cover in his back pocket. The remaining book of history.

I'm forgetting something.

That unnamed something nibbled at the back of his mind, even as he pushed through the crowd. Shaeda tried to pull him back, but the impulse to see this through was momentarily stronger.

A fleeting image of Thomas in the desert flashed across his mind.

"Such is madness, my Johnisss . . ."

He grabbed Cassak by the arm. "Those magic books in the attic. Did you ever find them?"

The man stared hard at him and yanked free. "I sent a man to look. The attic was cleared."

Johnis stiffened. Silvie's head snapped toward him. From seven to one in so short a space? "They were in a crate."

"We have not time for such indulgences, my pet . . ." Shaeda was getting impatient. She had absolutely no patience for anything not directly related to her purposes, her goals. Still, she was hiding something from him. Many somethings.

Silvie touched his shoulder, snapping him out of his trance.

Cassak shook his head. "I double-checked myself once I got around to it. The entire room was empty. Sorry."

Heart racing, Johnis followed the captain around the corner. He was confident, but Shaeda's anxiety grew as they neared the throne room. Her memories surfaced, memories of things the Shataiki—Derias—had done. Shaeda's terror wound around his heart and chilled him to the core.

"What was that about?" Silvie asked.

Johnis blinked. Shaeda cut off the connection. Her cold, tangible fear, though, lingered.

"Josef." Silvie pressed her fingers on his chest. "You are going to be rid of her? Her power, remember?"

Was he? Did he still desire to?

Life without Shaeda . . .

A low, menacing laugh sounded in his head.

Johnis froze. Then managed to clear his throat. "Not now." He changed the subject, hoping to throw Shaeda off, and possibly distract her fear. "What did Sucrow do to you?"

I can't do this with you strangling me, he protested. Her grip relaxed slightly.

Silvie didn't answer immediately. "He tortured me."

The priest and the general stopped abruptly and saluted four Scabs armed with spears who stood before the broad, white double doors that led into Qurong's throne room. The warriors saluted Marak and stepped to the side.

The doors swung open with a solid crash like thunder against the walls. Qurong's hall echoed, first with the sound of the doors, then again as the guards slammed their spear butts down in unison. Three times the sound pealed through the hall and rattled the fixtures, even Teeleh's winged-serpent image.

Shaeda braced herself. She recoiled at the sight of the idol. Johnis took a long, ragged breath and crossed the threshold.

DARSAL GAPED AT THE FAN-SHAPED ROOM THAT SPRAWLED before them. Red-robed warriors armed with swords and spears lined the wall. A chandelier with six rings, the widest easily eight feet across, hung full of dripping candles from the ceiling twelve feet above them. Hibiscus and broad-leafed gold hyling plants splashed orange, red, green, gold, and purple around the room and gave off a sweet scent that almost masked the stink of the Horde.

A long, purple carpet lined the center of the white stone floor and circled around and over a six-foot platform that served Qurong's throne. The high-backed chair was made of a reddish wood and covered in what looked like rich purple silk. Torch stands stood proud on either side.

And there sat Qurong, robed in blue and tan, with a gold necklace at his throat and his sword at his side. Long braids spilled down his back and over his shoulders. He sat tall and regal, every inch the great Horde leader. His cloak was off one shoulder and bared his right arm. A steward attended him. Qurong displayed only power and anger. If the Shataiki swarm unnerved him,

Darsal couldn't tell. He was a mean snake, and the bats had only seemed to make him meaner.

The Scabs bowed upon their approach. When Darsal did not, Marak gave her a look. She shook her head. He motioned her to stand out of sight.

Qurong scowled at his priest and his general, his expression mocking. "I see you've managed not to kill each other." He shifted forward, leaning as if to rebuke wayward children.

He said nothing of the Shataiki outside.

"Respectfully, lord," Marak said, his voice stiff. "Our mission is not complete."

"Oh, really?" The supreme commander leaned farther forward. A sneer split the morst on his face. "Then why are you here?"

Darsal glanced at Johnis, expecting him to answer. But his eyes had that purple cast to them, and he seemed pale.

Who was really in control?

Marak spoke. "We've four days to kill the albinos before the amulet's powers reverse. A day and a half has already passed."

"I repeat my original question then." Qurong scowled.

"My lord," Sucrow said, "we must journey to a high place in the northwest desert, in the mountains. The journey will take the majority of what little time remains. However, there is—"

"Then what are you still here for? Ride through the night if you must, but get rid of those albinos once and for all," Qurong snapped. He stood.

"Lord, there is one other thing . . ." Sucrow continued.

Qurong snarled. "What?"

"The ritual requires a small amount of blood. That is why we are here rather than continuing on our way—"

"My lord,"—Marak tensed—"it's your blood he and Josef insist they need. That is why he's dancing around like a child on an anthill."

Sucrow scowled at Marak.

"Excuse me?" Qurong roared.

"The ritual calls for the ruler of men to spill a portion of his blood," Sucrow explained. "It need not be more than a drop or two."

The Horde leader's eyes narrowed. He considered this for a long minute, then growled. "Very well. But do not try my patience again. When next I see your faces, the albinos had better be dead, down to the last squalling infant. You will leave immediately."

TWENTY-ONE

Darsal went with Marak to a guest room while Sucrow drew Qurong's blood, again with more pomp and ceremony than truly needed, thus turning five minutes into an hour. As though they had more time to lose. Let them lose time.

Perhaps it would spare the Circle. It would certainly give her more time.

She swept the room. Linen blankets, reed mats, more bright colors. A scribe's desk sat to the side, with Marak's original Desecration plans strewn over it. Martyn's war journal. Marak was keeping his plans as backup in case Johnis failed.

Marak stripped off his cloak and crossed the room to dig in his pack for morst. He stripped off his tunic, exposing rotting, flaking white flesh. A fresh gust of rotten-egg smell hit Darsal.

She grimaced at the sight of his back and looked away. She'd thought she was used to the sight of Scab skin but had never seen the full extent of the general's scabbing disease. An absolute beast. She tried hard not to gag.

He rubbed the white paste over his chest, arms, and neck, then as much of his back as he could reach. Watching him was painful.

And she remembered it wasn't only his skin that was diseased. His coarseness, his decision to kill the Circle, his execution of his family—all part of the Great Deception that ate away at his mind, soul, and body.

She cleared her throat. "Has Cassak gone to Qurong?"

No answer. Her general pulled his tunic back over his skin and drew his cloak over his shoulders. He put away the morst.

"Marak."

He didn't turn toward her, instead staring at the wall for a long minute. "Soon enough it won't matter."

Darsal furrowed her brow. "You don't mean that."

"Get me some water."

"It's right there on the table," she protested.

"I don't want that water." He went to his desk and studied something. He wouldn't look at her, and it was maddening.

Darsal knotted her fists. Marak was just being boneheaded, deflecting emotion by pulling rank, but now it was getting to her. "It's all the water there is, unless you feel like taking a side trip to a red lake."

"Darsal," he scoffed. "It's over. Don't you understand that?"

Deceived, she reminded herself. *He's deceived.*

"As soon as Sucrow reaches the high place, it's over for the Circle."

Elyon's love had no place in this hellhole, no seat of honor among snakes. Darsal slammed her fist on the wood. "Is this a game to you?" Marak's papers and notebook rattled. The tumbler sloshed over, and a thick, black mark streaked across the top page.

He jumped back. "Are you insane?"

She was going mad, acting like this. But they were out of time, and she was sick of dealing with him.

Marak raised his arms, glaring at the table. "What's wrong with you?"

"What do you think is wrong with me?"

His mouth clamped shut, and he took several long, heavy breaths, nostrils flaring. He finally broke his death glare and turned his back to her.

Darsal's anger exploded. The general's precious papers were all over the table. She gripped the edge and flipped the table. Everything went flying. "Don't turn your back on me!"

He didn't turn. He just stood there with his back to her, gawking at the mess without a word, cold and lifeless. A hacksaw tore its way through her body.

"Marak, you don't have to do this."

Elyon's gentle prodding suggested she relent. She wouldn't. Couldn't.

"Yes, I do need to do this, Darsal." Her general's voice deepened. "We're going to execute the albinos. All of them."

"Marak, *I'm* an albino!"

"I *know*!" He refused to look at her, instead surveying the strategies and plans strewn all over the floor, months of work that, if Johnis's plan worked, would amount to nothing.

The Desecration. He'd sold Jordan for that.

Darsal's heart sank into her shoes at his pronouncement. This ruthless Scab in front of her would never back down, even for love, because Elyon was not with him.

I'm sorry, Elyon. I can't do this anymore. I can't.

Marak righted the table, then the chair. His own temper was flaring, and he was doing his best to control it. She could tell by his slow, deliberate movements. It sobered her, shamed her, that he succeeded where she had failed.

"The thought of anyone living in that kind of pain drives me mad. I can't force anyone to live like that. That's why. And their minds . . . Darsal, I can't let that go on. I cannot."

His words grated at her. Darsal's fists knotted at her sides. Could she really give up on him?

Elyon wouldn't.

Heaven help them.

"That includes me."

Marak continued to clean up her mess. The man was ice. The comment hung in the air, thick and oppressive, just like the mass of bloodthirsty Shataiki outside.

"You're different," Marak whispered.

Darsal tried to rein in her temper. She reached out to put her hand on his shoulder. *Deceived. He is deceived, rotten to the core. He doesn't know . . .*

"I'm going to do my job." His voice sounded like piano strings pulled too tight. He wouldn't even look up, wouldn't turn and show her his face.

She withdrew her hand.

The general separated several wet pages and returned them to their proper places. Each movement was stiff, unnatural.

A thought crept into her mind, a desperate card she had no right to play. Darsal removed Jordan's pendant from her throat and placed it on top of the journal he was holding.

Marak was on his feet and in her face before she knew he'd turned around. "Leave my brother out of this! The lakes are poison, my people are getting sick and dying, and the albinos are to blame! And in under three days we'll have purged the world of their plague!"

"You really think your brother was a plague?"

The morst around his face had cracked. "I would rather you die than be an albino!"

"Then kill me!" Darsal grabbed one of Marak's writing journals and tore it at the spine. She ripped at the pages and scattered them across the room. Then she flung the ruined leather cover against the wall.

The cover splayed upside down, title showing.

A chilly noose tightened around Darsal's throat.

They both stared at the book, frozen in place for a minute.

Rona's journal.

She had destroyed it.

Darsal's hand went to her mouth.

Marak started around the room. He found each page of the journal, smoothed the creases out, and stacked them in order. He sank down and stared awhile longer, uncertain what to do with his recovered treasure.

Finally, he flipped over the remaining pages of the book, still bound, and tucked the shorn ones in the back. He placed the cover back in position and bound the whole mess together with twine. Then he set the book down and traced the leather with calloused fingers.

It was all he had left of Rona.

And Darsal had taken it from him.

"Marak."

He didn't respond. He'd forgotten she was in the room.

"I lost my temper. I'm sorry. I . . . I didn't mean . . ."

He did not blink. He did not move.

She stole forward, all her rage evaporated in an instant. Her eyes fell to the book's cover.

To Marak, with all my love.

Marak's hand spread over the writing. He looked up at her, eyes cold, gray, expressionless. Not even hate. Numbness overtook her.

Elyon, what have I done?

Someone knocked. "General, it's Cassak."

Marak didn't answer. Darsal stepped away from him, toward the door. "Enter, Captain." Her voice was dry, her throat parched.

The captain came in, saluted Marak, and surveyed the room. Jordan's Circle necklace was beneath Marak's foot. Cassak's eyes narrowed. "What happened in here?"

Still Marak didn't speak. Cassak's hawkish gaze turned on Darsal, accusing.

"Is Sucrow ready to leave?" Darsal asked sharply.

The captain's scowl deepened. He gave a short nod. "Sucrow sealed the blood in a vial. Qurong's given us leave to go. It's almost sundown."

Now Darsal and Cassak both stood waiting for Marak to say something.

Finally the captain said, "Go ready his horse."

Darsal blinked, then ran out the door, face hot. Marak didn't even yell after her.

TWENTY-TWO

Night fell over Middle, made darker by the swarming cloud above them. Sucrow looked up, fascinated and terrified all at once. Such a glorious sight, the silent shroud of Shataiki slowly drawing up over Middle, coming to cover them beneath black wings.

Sucrow's elite surrounded him, each Throater's robes glistening in the torchlight borne by his acolytes. Neither stars nor moon, merely the ruby-red eyes of his master's servants.

Soon, soon all would see the truth, even obstinate Marak.

"You've the book of rites?" Sucrow whispered as Warryn rode up alongside him. The tall serpent warrior gave a single nod. "Keep it close." His eyes narrowed in the direction of Marak and Josef. "I don't want it in the hands of infidels. And give the blood to one of the others. I'll not have any more tricks. Get the captain in place."

An hour out the scouts ahead slowed. Marak clucked to his horse and rode forward. His albino slave rode close, holding a torch for him to see. Her dark eyes fixed on Sucrow.

Sucrow cackled. "Lost already?"

"I'm not lost, General," the scout protested, making his appeal to Marak instead of Sucrow. "The bats block out the sky."

"Why don't you have a torch?" Sucrow demanded. "Am I surrounded by imbeciles?"

"A torch will not show me the stars," the scout snapped. "I'm trying to ride beyond the swarm, but they're fast. I sent three ahead and told them to loop back."

"What's wrong?" Josef rode up, brooding.

"Our illustrious priest doesn't seem able to comprehend the concept of scouting," Marak quipped. Sucrow bristled. To the scout Marak said, "Try to stay ahead of the swarm. And take another torch. What happened to yours?"

"I got caught in some mud and nearly fell into one of those foul red pools," the scout said.

Marak didn't comment.

"Well, get on with it," Josef scoffed. "There is no reason to stop."

That drew Marak's attention. "Blame the priest."

"It's your scout, I might remind you," Sucrow warned evenly. He scowled. This Josef would have to be done away with. The Master would not be pleased that such an unbeliever held his servants hostage. And Marak was in the way.

"And it's Josef's directions and your bloody ritual," Marak snapped. He sent the scout off. "We're wasting time."

Sucrow waited until Josef and Marak broke off. He called Warryn to him. "Wait until tomorrow," he said. "Then invoke the Law of Naroush."

A knowing look crossed the chief serpent warrior's face. The Law of Naroush was the cry for blood on behalf of a petitioner.

Josef had started them on this path. Surely he would not mind using his own blood to petition Teeleh's blessing.

ONCE MORE JOHNIS SAT ASTRIDE A HORSE, THIS TIME NORTH-bound on the west side of Middle. Once more into the unknown. If he looked back, he couldn't even see the city anymore; it was so consumed with the black cloud of Shataiki. The boiling cauldron was quiet. Johnis dropped back to Silvie.

Shaeda's cold talons dug into him. This many Shataiki so close made her nervous, despite her control over the swarm. She lingered in a hazy place between gloating and panicking. This, on top of Johnis's own apprehension, didn't help matters.

"You fear them more than I do," he whispered.

"Silence," she hissed. But her mind was open, thoughts set on her goal. They had conned the Shataiki amulet guardian and bound him. They would destroy the Horde and return victorious, and then she would be powerful enough to undermine Teeleh, to usurp his power and take it for her own.

Johnis blinked. Where had that come from?

"What was that all about?" Silvie's face was impossible to read.

"Sucrow being Sucrow."

Shaeda turned her focus to her missing mate, away from her plans for glory. She understood now. Silvie was to him as Rasmuth was to her.

Johnis's eyes flicked toward the enraged Derias. He'd taken Shaeda's mate, but Shaeda wouldn't explain everything about such.

How aware of the Leedhan's movements was Teeleh?

Sucrow, of course. Teeleh could guess through his priest.

So what would he do when . . .

Shaeda took his mind from those troubling thoughts.

Johnis fingered the amulet. So close, so close. And soon he would conquer the Horde and rule Middle with Silvie as his queen.

They reached a series of canyons and spread out to cross what otherwise was too narrow a path for the horses to pass through. A loud, snarling roar went up, spooking the horses.

"What's that?" one of the warriors asked.

Johnis's head whipped around. Shaeda completely balked. His nostrils flared. "Derias," he said, fingering the amulet around his neck. "He hasn't forgiven us for his imprisonment."

A flickering of fear snaked through him.

"We shall have accomplished our mission, yet upon its end what shall befall? The Guardian shall be full of wrath once he is released."

Johnis stiffened. "Shaeda, what do you mean?" he whispered.

Silvie looked at him. "What's wrong?"

He shook his head. What *would* Derias do once the amulet's powers were spent? They couldn't hold him forever—even Shaeda knew that.

"Have no fear," Shaeda soothed, as much to herself as to him. *"We will order his own termination ere this ends."*

The ritual that unlocked the amulet's power required Sucrow's presence. He alone knew the incantation. Only a priest of Teeleh could deliver the offering and approach the high place.

"Do you hear that?" Johnis whispered to Silvie. She eyed him. "Derias will kill us if we lose control of him before our mission is complete."

He grew uneasy. His entity was not telling him everything. Her dark presence came over him like a hot, thick blanket. He wasn't supposed to tell Silvie of his private conversations with the Leedhan monarch.

With Shaeda's night vision he could see Silvie fingering her knife. "Yes."

"Whatever happens, we cannot let the priest have the amulet."

Silvie was quiet a moment. Then, "So what do you want to do?"

"We need to plan."

THE SCOUTS REPORTED BACK TO MARAK CLOSE TO MIDnight. At least, that was his best estimation. The foursome traded off riding ahead and doubling back, a system that took them beyond the eclipse and beneath the stars.

"Past the canyons is a stretch of open desert," the lead scout told him, thumbing northwest. "If we turn west now, we'll bypass the foothills, then make north again along the rim. That'll take us to the peak."

"How long?" Marak snapped.

Easy, brother, he imagined Jordan saying, half-amused that Marak had let a girl get to him, and half-frustrated with Marak's tyrannical behavior since the fight with Darsal. *What did that scout do to you?*

Nothing, you bonehead.

But it didn't matter. It just didn't matter.

He caught himself fingering Jordan's Circle pendant.

"A few hours, General," the scout was saying. "The delay will be inconsequential. It would take longer to go through than around."

"You're certain."

The scout hesitated. "General—"

"We're ready to get this done. Tell the captain to follow your lead." The scout saluted him and galloped off.

"You kept it." Darsal's voice surprised and agitated him. They had barely spoken since she'd destroyed Rona's journal.

Marak's hand closed around the pendant. He put the necklace away. Thoughts of the pool mingled with those of the high place. He had the strange urge to break away from the others and ride until the horse dropped dead to the high place, to not wait for the priest or the others . . .

Focus, man.

"Sucrow has his hands in too deep," he said, changing the subject. "And what do you care?" Of course, he knew the answer as quickly as he asked it.

Darsal raised her torch higher and glimpsed in the direction of the enraged Shataiki queen. "I shouldn't have done that, General." General. In front of the men he was just "General." Behind their backs he was *her* general. Her Marak.

He snorted. "The albino admits she's wrong." Teeleh's breath, she destroyed everything, and now she was trying to dig in again.

She pursed her lips and waited for the apparent frustration to pass. "I was a fool."

He'd had some time to think about this. In some strange way the ripped journal knotted a loose thread, let him say good-bye. Tore the last of the barbs out of his heart.

Her horse drew abreast of his. Their knees brushed briefly. Heat shot up his leg. Marak threw her a look, eyes narrow. Darsal seemed not to notice. The torchlight gave her skin a strange cast, made it glow orange red.

His mind drifted again, just for a minute, just long enough to consider they could reach the high place so much faster with fewer men . . .

"Green for Elyon's lake," she said under her breath, just loud enough for his ears alone. Her voice brought him out of the wanderings. "Black for the Black Forest and the Great Deception. Red for the blood mingled with water."

He softened. "Jordan told you that."

"He did."

"And the white center?"

"Yet to come." Darsal moved a step ahead of him, looked up at the Shataiki swarm. "Sooner or later."

"Albino." The word came out more sharply than Marak had intended. He caught up to her. She glanced over, then turned her eyes forward again. Marak hesitated. He wanted to keep it. Now it really was all he had left.

"Get out of my blind spot," she corrected quietly. It was one of the first things he'd said to her when he'd taken her to his home as a slave.

Marak drew a breath, then offered it to her. "It means more to you than me."

She managed a half smile. "I think he'd want you to keep it."

"He gave it to you."

"But not to keep." Darsal spurred her horse and rode well ahead of everyone but the scouts.

Sucrow shouted after her. "Marak, get ahold of your bloody albino!"

Marak pocketed his brother's necklace before anyone could notice. "She's on orders, Priest. Let her alone."

The priest fumed and threatened, but Marak's attentions were lost. A sense of dread washed over him. With every step toward the high place, it increased. After an hour with no sight of Darsal and the gnawing still in his gut, Marak called Cassak to him.

They studied each other, remnants of a friendship scarcely there. Cassak rubbed a spot on his neck, a strange habit he'd picked up over the last few days.

"The Eramites relocated," the captain reported. "They reached the base of the foothills, turned around, and went back south."

"Did something spook them?" Marak's stomach knotted. Cassak had stolen from him once; what else might he do?

"Nothing that we've seen. But we did find a few stripped skeletons, both horse and human." Suspicion clouded the captain's eyes. Marak could tell there was a lingering question his old friend wanted to ask but wouldn't. Probably about Darsal's running off. She'd likely left to let Marak think. As for Cassak, he had always used indirect methods to communicate and came to his point at his own leisure.

But that Cassak Marak no longer knew.

"Jackals?" he asked.

Cassak's expression turned dark. "Marak, I don't think a jackal could do this."

His first impulse was to look skyward, but he resisted. Knew already. Instead Marak looked long at the priest, then in the direction Darsal had gone. Something was wrong. Darsal was missing, Cassak was behaving strangely, and Marak could not shake his foul mood. He felt like a Throater.

"Find out."

Unease settled in. A slow draw toward the high place, a desire to hurry, seeped over him. He needed to get to the high place. He needed to keep an eye on the priest.

"General." Marak blinked. Cassak was still standing there, waiting.

"Well, go," Marak snapped.

TWENTY-THREE

The sky ahead was gradually turning from gray to purple, just barely hinting at the dawn of morning. Behind them, abysmal black dotted with red engulfed everything in its path. The Shataiki cauldron boiled hot, its queen raging from somewhere within the throng. Faster they flew, blotting out those last wisps of light from beyond. The mere sight made Shaeda's—Johnis's—skin crawl.

The scouts led the expedition party out of the canyons and west across open desert. Not exactly according to plan, but not hindering either. This way they would have less climbing this afternoon.

Shaeda's anticipation mounted. She hadn't punished his thoughts of keeping her powers, and he began to think she'd forgotten, not heard, or forgiven him.

Yes, that was right.

Wasn't it?

Her prompting led him to the front of the pack, along the left flank, away from the others. Of course he would go. Why would he not? Idly he fingered the amulet in their hands. He licked his lips. Oh, yes, the time was nigh. He had overpowered and enslaved this queen, and now he would do Shaeda's will. Teeleh would be pleased, very pleased.

"Joh . . . sef." Silvie rode up beside him, her pale eyes narrow. "Where are you going?"

Johnis's mind snapped into focus. He glanced at her. Silvie had found a piece of flint and now sharpened her daggers to thin, lethal edges. She remained skeptical. "You're too far ahead."

Irksome female. Why did she have to nag at him like that? Johnis's brow furrowed. "The scout reported carrion. I was looking into it."

Silvie's expression indicated she didn't believe him. She scanned the desert floor. The Shataiki hive was overhead now, and once more they could see little. Johnis rode forward.

"And you saw nothing?" she asked.

"Still looking. My concern was feeding bats."

"Marak and the priest will be angry."

He studied Silvie. Shaeda's talons stroked his neck, tickling his skin. He'd allowed her presence to dominate his since the slip. But she was getting stronger. With all his senses on such high alert and firing in his body, he felt like a madman. He saw her eyes, her beautiful, intoxicating eyes . . .

Shaeda came over him. Her strength became his.

Her will . . . her mind . . .

Johnis's back—Shaeda's back—arched. Prepared to strike.

"Johnis?" The brief silhouette rode toward them.

Darsal approached, her torch high. Sweat glistened on her face, streaking morst and exposing smooth, dark skin.

Johnis scowled. Shaeda bristled. His vision turned hazy. They were done with this albino. Shaeda wanted her blood.

But Johnis restrained the impulse first. Not now, not when in a matter of hours it wouldn't matter who killed the wench.

"What do you want?" Silvie demanded.

The albino's gaze swept from Silvie to Johnis.

"Help. We're almost out of time. You really want to kill the Guard? Make an alliance with a Shataiki?"

Silvie's jaw hardened. "What do you know?"

Johnis narrowed his eyes.

"More than you think." Darsal's voice was strained. Desperate. Of course she was desperate. As soon as Sucrow performed the ceremony and Johnis gave the order, she was dead. Johnis would make sure of that.

"Johnis, do you know what the Circle is?"

He snorted, fingered his ring. "My name is Josef."

"Josef is bound to a Leedhan. You are Johnis. You are Johnis who forgave me. Remember that."

He saw only a swarm of bats and blood mingling in water.

Shaeda showed her teeth.

Darsal jabbed her finger in his face. "Your mother would not tolerate you killing hundreds of our own people because she was murdered. I didn't know her long, but I know that much!"

"You know nothing!" Johnis rose up in the saddle. "You don't talk about her. You don't even speak her name."

"The Circle is your mother. It is me. You and Silvie."

A surge of heat billowed deep in his gut and worked its way up through his chest and down his arms. "You have no business talking to me this way," he growled. Darsal was in the way of the mission. She'd served her purpose.

Shaeda wanted to kill the albino. Here. Now. Johnis craved Darsal's blood.

No!

"You are a doomed slave, and I am the next ruler of Middle."

Darsal drew her horse close and put her hand on his leg. "You can defeat Sucrow without the amulet, without Shaeda. You've never needed magic or anything but the brain Elyon gave you."

She'd grabbed him like that before.

That Darsal.

He kicked, then swung his sword at her, broadside. She hit the ground and rolled sideways, limbs sprawled, groaning from her injuries. The horse squealed and barely avoided crushing her.

"Go back to your precious Scab. You're already dead."

Darsal struggled to rise. "Silvie, tell him! You know it's absurd to think that siding with Sucrow or the bats is a good idea."

"Leave her out of this," Johnis snapped. Shaeda was going to pounce. He was going to tear Darsal to shreds.

"She's already in it." Darsal made it to her feet.

"It is my kisses he prefers," Shaeda said through Johnis's mouth. Her laughter overtook him.

"Excuse me?" Silvie snapped.

Johnis fought for control. What was she doing, telling the girls that?

But he had liked Shaeda's kisses, hadn't he?

Shaeda chuckled.

"She kissed you?" Darsal turned on him, completely stunned. She grabbed Silvie's reins. "Since when have you let anyone but Silvie kiss you?"

"You're just trying to divide us. I love Silvie, and that's final."

"Final as using black magic to overpower the Shataiki and destroy everything we all bled and died and sacrificed for. Is it that final, Johnis?"

He threw Silvie a look. She jumped off the horse and on top of Darsal, then pinned her, arm behind her back. Darsal wrestled free and struck Silvie broadside. She hit the ground, unconscious.

Johnis snarled.

"You're as certain as my death that those bats are completely under your control? That they will not and cannot betray you?"

"They are bound to the medallion. I could have a throng of them kill you now, right here."

"Tell me something, O mighty Chosen One. What makes you

think that after you destroy the Circle and destroy everyone you hate, they'll leave the Scabs alone? They'll do what you command, Johnis, and more, just like last night. They defied the boundaries once; they'll do it again. And you and Silvie will wind up bat food, like the rest of us."

Shaeda poured into him. He knew he was transforming. Again. He was becoming Leedhan.

"You're wrong."

"I pray to Elyon I am. Remember him? Teeleh hates him. Teeleh hates you too. Tried to kill you once. Open your eyes, Johnis. You're going to destroy what you love the most."

She had a point, didn't she? They were going to use Shaeda's power to turn tables on the Leedhan, to somehow turn the bats on the Horde . . .

"The albino poisons you," Shaeda rebuked. The transformation completed. *"She wishes your destruction. She will destroy our true mission . . ."*

"Johnis, you stubborn fool, listen to me!"

Shaeda exploded. They sprang at Darsal and slammed her against the ground. Tore at the albino's throat. Darsal thrashed from under Johnis, rammed into the horse. She knocked his pack off. Water and food splattered across the desert sand.

"Johnis!" Darsal went into a crouch and sought a weapon. Her eyes found the horse.

Shaeda—inside Johnis—pounced on the albino. Darsal barely dodged her, rolled. Johnis caught her by the shoulder. Darsal clawed at his hand and struck him hard in the face, wrenched loose. She tore the reins from one of the bridles and snapped them like a whip.

Their blood mingled with the water, stained the desert sand.

"Shaeda," Darsal snapped, "let him go!"

Shaeda hissed. Johnis's lip curled.

"Kill her."

"Kill her now and we lose Marak," Johnis growled. He gasped for breath. Shaeda's energy taxed him. Darsal had torn a hunk of flesh out of him.

Silvie stirred from the ground. In the end Shaeda would kill Silvie, wouldn't she? Darsal was right. He was destroying the very thing he loved.

Did his heart really desire to kill the Circle?

Kill Silvie and Darsal?

Shaeda was not rational when she gave way to her hate. Her talons dug into him, punishing his contradiction. And now she knew her pet would never be wholly hers.

Darsal didn't lower the leather rein serving as her whip. "Let him go," she repeated.

Hoofbeats pounded toward them from the foothills.

Throaters. Hair on end, Johnis turned. Five of them. His blood ran cold. Why hadn't he foreseen this? Why hadn't Shaeda—

Talons tore into him. Leedhan fury bore down on his shoulders, almost knocked him off balance. "Shaeda, what are you—"

"Let him go!" Darsal screeched.

"I do not tolerate weakness," Shaeda warned between Johnis's teeth. His knees buckled.

I am not weak!

"You have not given me your heart."

Darsal turned and met the Throaters head-on. Warryn caught her across the throat with a spear shaft and sent her flying. She hit with a disgusting thud.

"Foolish albino."

Silvie was throwing a fit. Johnis found his sword and invoked Shaeda's power. Nothing. The Throaters fell on Silvie and struck her hard across the skull. Johnis lunged, then hit the ground and rolled, medallion in his fist.

Shaeda!

He crossed blades with the Throater. The Leedhan hissed in his ear, all her strength, all her power pouring out of him. As she left, the full weight of everything she had sustained him through bore down on him. He had neither eaten nor slept. He'd ridden for days on end. He'd fought, he'd run, he'd—

Johnis went down, sword clattering. Desperate, groping for the medallion. A heavy boot stomped on his hand and took it from him. The Throater sneered. Someone flipped him on his belly and bound his wrists and ankles.

Shaeda wanted his heart and could not have it. Now she would let the priest have him. Johnis's mind began to swim. Heavy fog surrounded him, blurred his vision.

The Throaters were talking, but Johnis could barely understand them, even as they dragged him up and slung him across the back of a horse as if he were a deer carcass.

"We'll deal with it," said Warryn. "Let the general handle his slave."

TWENTY-FOUR

Darsal woke to the end of a spear shaft probing her. She groaned and rolled away from the intrusion. Where . . . ?

Eyes opening, she saw reddish-brown desert and warm blood drying on a rock. Everything came crashing back: Johnis, Shaeda, Silvie, the Throaters, Warryn . . .

She jumped into a crouch and spun.

"Easy, albino." Cassak had dismounted and glared at her, still holding his spear. Behind him his horse stamped and shied, nervous. He spat. "I should have talked the general into executing you."

"Talked him into it?" How dare he talk about Marak like that. Darsal raised a brow, scanned the ground, heart pounding. This wasn't the Cassak loyal to Marak—who would spare her for his friend's sake.

The starry-eyed serpent at his throat seemed to come alive.

"We could find out what he thinks of that." Her blood and Johnis's had already soaked into the dirt. The horses were gone. The Throaters, Johnis, and Silvie were all gone. Were they dead? Had Warryn taken them somewhere?

"He knows what I meant." The captain seemed pensive, though, as if he hadn't intended it the way it sounded after all. What was Sucrow using him for?

"I really don't have time to argue."

Behind Cassak the rest of the expedition party was coming, a black shroud of Shataiki in the lead. All was gray and black, riddled with beady, glowing red.

What had Warryn done to them?

Elyon's words nibbled at the back of her mind. She felt her heart straining in two. Darsal was being spiteful, and she knew it. At the moment she wasn't sure she cared. But she loved them, didn't she? Even Marak's captain.

She forced herself to soften. *Love the Horde.*

"I think you do. What's happened here?" the captain demanded. He traded his spear for his sword. Darsal kept her palms extended. She'd taken Johnis's knife, but the Throaters must have taken it away from her, thought her dead. Why didn't Cassak just run her through?

Because Marak wouldn't want him to. That knowledge would work to her advantage. Part of the captain still struggled against the enchantment. Her mind raced for an answer.

"I was looking for water," she snapped. "Is that a crime?"

Easy, Darsal.

Why should she be? This man would kill her were it not for Marak's orders, and Marak had every intention of allowing the priest to kill all of them.

Return to the Horde and love them for me. For Johnis.

She pushed back the gentle reminder.

"There was a fight," he said.

"The priest's Throaters are a pack of jackals." Darsal's brow went up again. She crossed her arms, then remembered this captain had hated the priest at one point. She wondered how much he hated Warryn, chief of the Throaters. Maybe if she could get to the bottom of Cassak's enchantment, she could give Marak his best friend and most trusted officer back.

She had never lied to Marak, and he was impressed by that. Impressed that he could trust her, a sworn enemy. And Cassak and Marak were made of the same cloth.

So she told the truth.

"Warryn attacked us. Sucrow's making a power play." She frowned. "Marak doesn't know about it. Did you?"

Cassak tensed. He rubbed his neck. "Where are Josef and Arya?"

"Tied to a cactus, for all I know. I need to find them before Warryn kills them. Remember Warryn, the one who made you watch him torture your best friend's family?" Her heart was in her throat. *I'm sorry, Marak. I don't have a choice.* Darsal thrust out a hand. "Lend me a knife, in case the Throaters come back. I'll return it."

The captain's eyes narrowed.

"I swear by Elyon." *And on the books.* "And I won't tell anyone where I got it, either."

"General would know."

Darsal stared at him. The man was split in two. One side showed her concern out of loyalty to Marak. The other seemed to despise everything he and Marak once held in common.

"What's Sucrow done, Captain? Are you really going to punish your best friend for what never was? Turn your back on him to serve a man you despise? That's what Josef's done. And it's killing him."

He hesitated. Darsal snatched his knife and ran. Cassak grabbed her collar. "Get back here, you little—"

"So you won't get in trouble." She punched him in the face, swung onto his horse, and galloped off.

JOHNIS BUCKLED IN PAIN. THE WORLD SEEMED TO SWIM, and everything was fuzzy. He tried to open his eyes but couldn't see more than a blur. Tried to move, but his cold, stiff muscles wouldn't cooperate. Sand kissed his cheek.

"Such a weakling you've proven, Chosen One. Such a pity . . ."

"Bloody fool," said a familiar voice that Johnis couldn't place.

Another kick to his already broken ribs. His head rose up against his will. A potent drink that smelled like Rhambutan and eggs slid down his throat. Bitter, hot liquid flooded his mouth.

Johnis gagged and tried to spit it up.

"None of that, now," said his tormentor. The rebuke came with a sharp blow to the side of his throbbing skull.

He swallowed. Shaeda . . . Where was Shaeda?

She'd left him. Abandoned him to the priest she despised. Had she planned this all along? Johnis rolled his head back and let out a groan.

"Foolish son of Ramosss . . . Did you truly believe I would remain with one so powerless? Nay, my pet . . . there are much larger trophies than you in poor Middle."

"Silvie . . . Silvie, where are you?" His voice echoed.

More voices.

"'Silvie, Silvie!'" Shaeda taunted. *"That leech has passed into the nether realm. Since you will not fully aid me, I will not allow her to live. Nor you, my unchosen one."*

A whip lashed across his bared, flaking skin. Johnis opened his mouth to scream, but no sound came out. He struggled, but his limbs rebelled against his will.

A cord wound around his neck and pulled taut, strangling him.

He sputtered and coughed, writhed on the ground. It felt like someone was dragging him over a bed of nails or hot coals. Johnis screamed this time. Laughter answered him.

"Pitiful son of Ramosss . . . Thomas would be so displeased . . . So disappointed that his best was far too weak . . ."

Johnis lost consciousness and dreamed, dreamed he was

underwater, hunted by a creature and devoured alive. The beast gave one last gulp, and Johnis slid into the hot, acidic blackness.

"Wake up!"

Johnis groaned and rolled over, startled to realize he could. His body felt torn to shreds. And maybe it was. The hand shook him. "I said wake up!"

Someone helped him sit up and tried to give him water. He turned his head to the side, but they grabbed his jaw and forced him to drink it. Warm, muddy water mixed with some kind of citrus slid down his throat.

"You're worse than your wench." His captor cackled.

Why are you doing this?

"I have spoken, my Johnisss . . . I require a more formidable ally, one whose loyalties are wholly mine . . . Farewell . . ." Shaeda laughed.

Johnis's head cleared a little, enough to know his arms were bound behind his back and his ankles secured painfully against each other. A bloody gash oozed on the side of his head, and needle pricks of pain drilled into his arms and legs. His rib cage felt crushed.

"I'm not sure who screams louder, you or the wench," the taunt continued. "She broke easily enough. We'll see about you."

He struggled to breathe, and on top of the rotten egg, citrus, and Rhambutan juice, he smelled a sickly sweet substance that dominated his senses above all else.

Johnis shook his head and opened his eyes. He was in the

desert, surrounded by Throaters. Warryn was the speaker. Sucrow had the medallion. Silvie . . . Where was Silvie?

Shaeda . . . Shaeda, wait! You gave your word!

Warryn snickered. "So you haven't died yet. Pity."

Johnis pursed his bloodied lips. He scanned the ground. Before him was a pit, a yawning gash in the ground, just deep enough that if he were thrown in, he wouldn't be able to climb out. But Silvie . . .

The Throater struck him across the side of the head, then cackled. "Such a pretty thing, the girl was."

Johnis snarled and lunged, then realized his wrists were over his head. "If you've touched Silvie . . ."

"I really don't care." Warryn raked his nails over Johnis's face and drew blood. Johnis swallowed the coppery-tasting liquid and too-salty saliva.

"Where is Silvie?"

Warryn leered. "Regrettably, she didn't last very long."

"I want to see her!" Johnis pushed up with his elbows but couldn't find any leverage. Someone kicked him down. His shoulder popped. Johnis grimaced.

"There's really nothing there you'll want to see."

"I want to see her." Johnis's stomach rebelled on him. He couldn't make himself believe that Silvie was dead. The Throater was lying; he had to be.

"What did you do to her?"

Warryn dragged Johnis up by the chain that tethered his

arms together and laughed in his face. "I'll leave her fate to your imagination."

Johnis started to protest, but Warryn flung him into the pit. The chain went taut and snapped his shoulders out of place. All his weight was suspended on his joints. He nearly passed out from the pain.

Johnis glared up at the Throater, looked for any source of leverage. He tried to grab the chain but couldn't.

Warryn left him, still gloating, no doubt. Johnis forced himself to breathe. He was in a hole . . . in the ground. A grave.

TWENTY-FIVE

"Where are they?" Marak was in Sucrow's face. He hadn't taken Sucrow's divulgence well. Josef and Arya were dead; Marak's precious albino had abandoned him.

The general really needed to mind his priorities.

Sucrow sneered, amused at the general's outrage. He had considered lying to Marak, but in some ways this was better. Sucrow twisted the staff in his hand and fingered the amulet beneath his tunic. Warryn had done better than Sucrow anticipated, which pleased him. At the moment his chief serpent warrior was likely making up his grievance with the Eramites the previous week.

Now, how would Marak respond to his captain's betrayal?

"Are you more concerned about the loss of extra baggage, General," Sucrow cackled, "or the loss of your albino and the amulet?" Dark tendrils sifted from his staff to Marak's neck, constricting. Marak rubbed the spot unwittingly.

Sucrow extended his hand to his servant and accepted the second jar of blood. The Chosen One's blood.

Marak's white eyes sized Sucrow up, no doubt considering tearing him apart. Morst cracked across his face and dripped down his cheeks and neck.

The general fingered his sword.

Sucrow laughed. "Do you really believe that sword will be of any use against me, Marak? I am Teeleh's high priest, and the amulet is back where it rightfully belongs. I have had power beyond comprehension for longer than you have been alive, and this is the greatest charm I have ever known. So you tell me how you think you will fare with two million of my lord's faithful at my back."

As if in answer, Derias gave out an agitated roar as the edge of the eclipse passed over them. Sucrow chanced a glimpse, still awed at the presence of so great a beast. *Soon,* he thought. *Soon you will be released from your prison.*

Marak snarled a minute longer, hand still on his sword. "Ride," he snapped, quickening the pace.

Sucrow spurred his own mount, still considering the amulet. "As soon as this is over, General," he promised, "Teeleh's servants will feast on you as well."

MARAK GALLOPED AHEAD OF THE OTHERS, NO LONGER willing to run alongside the priest but compelled to ride out to this high place as swiftly as possible and be done with the matter. The black horde above prodded him on.

Beneath his tunic, Jordan's pendant bounced against his chest. Why he was wearing it, he'd never explain to the others. But why shouldn't he wear his brother's necklace?

Forget it. And Darsal. Above all, forget Darsal. A knot formed in his stomach.

"General!" A figure on foot waved. As his mount's pounding hooves carried him closer, Marak saw his captain, blood and dirt smeared over him. No knife. Cassak fumed.

Marak drew up on the reins, circled his captain. "Where's your horse?" He pulled up and glanced back. The dark shadow was already over them, and Sucrow would be only minutes behind.

"Your albino," Cassak snapped. "She knocked me out and took my knife and my horse and rode off to Teeleh knows where. Cursed wench."

Marak bristled at the slur and felt the knot in his gut tighten.

"She left," the captain accused. "She ran like a bloody coward."

Marak didn't respond.

Cassak snatched the reins and jerked the horse's head around. "I told you this would happen. I sent men after her. If she fouls this up, Marak—"

Marak snatched the reins free of his captain. "She can't foul it up, Cassak. Josef and Arya are dead. Sucrow has the amulet. I have the army. Why don't you tell me how one unarmed woman knocks you out and takes your knife right out of your belt?"

One of the scouts raced back to him and saluted. "General, we've located the Ba'al Bek. Also, Eram's search parties—"

"Give the captain a fresh horse," Marak barked at him. He scowled at Cassak, awareness of their breaking—already broken—friendship settling on his shoulders.

The scout dismounted and offered his reins to the captain. "I run fast enough, sir." Normally the gesture would have been immediately rewarded, but Marak was too frustrated to bother responding to it.

To Cassak, Marak ordered, "Take ten and clear out the rebels. Don't tell them anything."

The brusque charge stunned Cassak, and for a moment he just stared. Then he gave a crisp salute and swung onto the scout's horse. He shouted at the beast and was gone.

The eclipse now completely overshadowed them. Derias's howl drowned out everything. Marak glanced back and saw the priest signaling him. He let Sucrow catch up.

"General, there is—"

"Last leg. Try to keep pace." Marak slapped the reins, knocking foam off horseflesh.

TWENTY-SIX

Darsal rode through the desert, praying to Elyon she would find Johnis and Silvie alive. She kept her course toward the high place, guessing that Warryn would plan to rejoin Sucrow and the other Throaters once he'd finished with his prisoners.

Two million Shataiki blacked out the sky and made time impossible to determine. She searched for Cassak's water bottle and drank from it, then grimaced. Horde water was anything but clean.

Somewhere beneath the canopy, one hundred warriors, twenty Throaters, Marak, and the priest were headed for the high place.

A cold, numb sensation swept over her. Darsal shook it off. On this path around the foothills, Warryn could find plenty of places to dump bodies and still reach his master quickly, she surmised.

Don't think that.

Still, the gnawing understanding that Johnis and Silvie were most likely dead, combined with the knowledge that she'd probably ruined any chance of winning Marak's love, wouldn't leave her. She felt the coarse, grating pain down to her bone and marrow.

Her mission had failed, and they were all dead.

Several hours passed, and still no sign. Her torch burned out, leaving her in the unnatural darkness. Darsal stayed her course, headed now into the foothills where the race was on. Marak and Sucrow would follow the scouts' advice and go around along the easier trail. But Darsal would cut through, and she was alone.

Assuming she was still heading north.

"Follow the bats," she grumbled to no one.

The horse startled. Darsal shouted and yanked his head down, pulled him in a tight circle. "Easy," she snapped. "Two million Shataiki and now you decide to—"

"Didn't mean to spook him," said a familiar voice. Darsal whipped her head toward Gabil, who slapped the air with his wings and lighted in front of her in the saddle. His green eyes stared up at her. "But you're going the wrong way."

"I'm going north," Darsal fired back. She heard the Shataiki queen's snarl from above, but when she looked up, she could see nothing but a black sea of the swarming beasts.

"Well, yes. But Marak's ahead of you now."

Darsal cracked the reins and got the horse moving again. The motion unsettled Gabil and made his wings flutter as he rebalanced himself.

"How far?"

"Half a mile or so. Not too far. But that isn't what I meant. You see—"

"Where are Johnis and Silvie?"

Gabil cocked his head. "I thought your mission was Marak."

"My mission is the Horde. To woo and win their love for Elyon. And I failed. My only choice is to try to find Johnis and get out of this mess." It sounded foolish when she said it, though. "I can't take on two million Shataiki, Gabil. Even you can't do that."

The Roush was slow to answer. "Well, true, but who told you to take on two million Shataiki, Darsal?"

"I can run a blade through their priest easily enough," she snarled. "If I reach them in time." Yes, that was a good plan, now that she thought about it. "Just tell me where Johnis and Silvie are, and point me through the mountains."

"You know I can only do so much, child."

He sounded more like Michal just then, and that unnerved her.

"How do you plan to drown them?" he asked at last.

"I'll figure it out."

"And Marak?"

"I broke his heart. It's over."

Gabil glanced up at the Shataiki swarm, then back at Darsal. "So that's it?"

"Human love only goes so far. Johnis, Gabil. Johnis."

"But Johnis isn't—"

"I am not going to talk about Marak." She fought the urge to knock him clean off the horse. But that would be foolish. Gabil was trying to tell her something, and she didn't like where he was going.

"I'm out of time with him," she insisted.

"Well, I don't know where they've taken Johnis and Silvie," Gabil admitted. "However, I don't think you'll succeed unless you first love the Horde."

"Love them." Darsal scoffed. "I tried. I've been patient."

Gabil chuckled. "Patient for you, yes."

She started to argue, then thought better. "You have a point. But that isn't helping me." Darsal studied him. A memory surfaced. She drew up short. "That's why you're here. I said all along the Shataiki will kill them all, Horde and Circle. It's true, isn't it?"

Gabil listened.

"I'm not going to find Johnis out here, am I?"

"You might. You might not."

She scowled.

"But you can find Marak."

Darsal tensed.

Gabil continued. "But the question remains: will you be patient a little longer, or do you wash your hands of him?" A pause. "You think you love him more than Elyon?"

She started to protest, but instead accepted his gentle rebuke.

"You think you love Johnis and Silvie more than Elyon? Or do you wash your hands of them as well? You're all quite stiff-necked."

Darsal glanced up at the sky, which was no longer visible.

Thunder pealed with the sharp crack of lightning. "I need a pool, Gabil. I can't find one in the dark." Even as she said it, she knew what she was going to do.

She still loved Marak, and Marak couldn't die a Scab.

A screech overhead. Shataiki wings slapped the air and circled over the peaks. The scouts.

Marak the Scab would never change his mind. But Marak the albino might.

Elyon save us.

The Roush laughed softly. "You'll always find water when you need it, Darsal. Trust that much. Elyon didn't bring you out here to die."

Another memory surfaced, and with it came understanding. Darsal drew a breath. Marak would be back with the rest of the expedition, headed north. She'd gone east a ways, looking for Johnis and Silvie, before turning north. Now she'd have to turn back west a bit to intercept the general.

No, Gabil said they'd passed her. Fine. Even more easily done.

But if Sucrow was making a power play, what would he do to Marak?

She'd find out . . .

"I leave them and find Marak, then. So be it." With those words came an ache.

A loud rush of leather wings and Shataiki roars split the air. The swarm circled twice in formation, endless rows and columns of glowing red eyes.

Gabil nodded. He flapped twice and was airborne. "Now, if you'll excuse me . . ."

"Wait, you're leaving again?"

"Two million Shataiki, Darsal. Neither of us is doing this alone. I would keep north, if I were you."

"WE WILL CUT THROUGH THE PASS," SUCROW SAID TO Marak's commander. "Spread the word." He gestured at two of his serpent warriors, who rode up on either side of the officer.

"Marak will be expecting us to follow the scout's advice," Reyan argued. "He'll be waiting."

"Is your general here?" Sucrow snapped. The commander tensed. "Inform your men that Marak has deserted to the rebels, and I am in command."

Reyan scowled. His hand fell to his scabbard, but Sucrow held up his hand. He twisted his fingers around his staff and silently invoked Teeleh's powers, already at hand. The commander's expression tensed. Tendrils of crimson slithered around Reyan's throat. Not that the commander would notice.

Sucrow flashed a wicked grin. If only this fool knew what was coming. "Come, now, Commander. Marak led you into the desert, only to desert in the final hours. I have equal rank with the general, if not higher, and it is to me you will look."

The commander's jaw tightened. "Marak's angry. Nothing more."

A fighter, then. As formidable as Cassak was, though the captain was more stubborn. So be it. If Reyan's will would not bend, it would break.

"Are you so certain?" Bile rose in Sucrow's throat. The general's mantra of loyalty, integrity, and honor had poisoned the entire army. A disgusting parasite he would soon rid them of. Sucrow dipped his staff.

Confusion drifted across the commander's face, just as surely as Sucrow's enchantment did its work. Reyan started to reply.

A rider in full gallop rushed straight for them. The scout raced straight across, heading for the front of the line. Their horses reared. The rider swerved in with a whoop, trying to knock them all off course.

Sucrow swung his staff. The rider grabbed the end and swung it level across his throat. Sucrow fell off the horse and landed on his back with the assailant on him. The smell hit him—an albino.

"Kill her, you fools!" he screamed, clawing at the albino. Three swords rang out. A hot knife blade dug into his throat, a thin trickle of blood forming below it.

"I'll kill him first! Where is Marak, Priest?" the general's slave growled. "What did you do with him? He's supposed to be here!"

Sucrow sneered. "What do you care?"

She leaned in close and whispered. "Three seconds, Priest. They can't kill me before I slit your throat."

"He deserted," Reyan snapped. "He left."

"Where, you half-brained dimwit?"

"North," Sucrow sneered. "Not that any of this will save you."

"It isn't about me." She grabbed him and swung back onto her horse, Sucrow slung across like a carcass. "Follow me and he dies! Ya!" The albino whipped the horse into a gallop and raced away from them.

Sucrow struck at her. She beat him over the head. "The medallion," she snapped. "Where is it?"

He snarled. "You're mistaken if you think I'd tell you."

"I could just search your clothes after you're dead."

Sucrow mentally began an incantation.

The albino turned the horse, taking a zigzag pattern to throw him off. The sky was almost too dark to see. The albino searched his clothes. Sucrow's hand clamped down around the amulet.

She tried to wrestle it from him. Sucrow sliced his sharp nails into her flesh. She fought with him. They both fell off the horse and hit hard. Sucrow snarled and raised his hands, clawlike.

"Your magic will not aid you," she snapped.

Sucrow didn't answer. He'd nearly killed her with a well-placed invocation before. He summoned Teeleh's power into his hands. An orb formed.

She dodged the blast and swung back onto the horse, then galloped into the mountains, presumably after her arrogant general.

The fools could both die out there. The Shataiki would have both of them.

The commander caught up to him, bringing the priest's horse and his staff. He mounted.

"She escaped."

"She won't escape for long." Sucrow motioned to his serpent warriors. The nearest ran his spear through Reyan and knocked him off his horse. Sucrow watched idly. "Never betray your master, Commander." He sneered. "Tragically, the albino killed you."

To his men, "Summon the captain. Inform him his general has deserted and his commander is dead. We must make haste to the high place before the albino does something foolish."

TWENTY-SEVEN

Marak guided his horse into the pass, following the scout's advice. From here he could see the precipice, the mountain where everything would end. He'd had enough of the priest, no desire to see him again before the ceremony, and certainly not after.

Idiot, why did you leave? he imagined Jordan demanding. *You left the priest unattended. Do you realize what he can do while you're gone? He already killed Josef. He has the medallion, brother.*

He knew, and his reason told him he needed to turn back, to stop following this insane compulsion to reach the peak ahead of Sucrow. Something was there, something he needed to get to before Sucrow. As important as the amulet itself.

A loud roar erupted from the mountain, underscored by the lightning storm that had started a half hour or so ago. When the light flashed again, Marak glimpsed the massive amulet guardian circling the high place, raging against his enslavement. A mere mortal had tricked him; no wonder he was so angry.

Marak shook his head, not sure how he knew such things or why he speculated them. The horse faltered, and he carefully set the animal's course on better footing.

"How in Teeleh's name is this faster?" he grumbled. The scout had to be mad.

"Marak!" A voice echoed over the wind. "Marak! Wait!"

Darsal?

He balked, looked over his shoulder. She was back?

Impulse took over. She'd ripped his heart out. Marak turned his back and kept going at a steady pace. Darsal called out again, making her way toward him as fast as the narrow drop-off allowed. Shataiki screeched and boiled above them, frothing at the mouth, Derias howling louder than all. Marak's senses were at their end, worn ragged by the chase.

His emotions twisted at the sound of her voice, at the smell of albino caught in the wind. Impulse drove him forward while his heart said to wait, to pull back, to let her catch him, to sweep her off her mount and hold her.

Darsal caught up to him. She rode up the side of the ravine and back down in front of him. Her hand lashed around his mount's reins. "Come with me!"

For a second he could only stare at her. Marak jerked on the leather. "I thought you left."

"Sucrow tried to kill us," she said. "I went after Warryn, but I didn't find him! We have to leave now!" She pulled the reins free of his hands and hurried the horses.

"Darsal!"

"Hurry!"

The bats were screaming above the mountains.

Darsal got them through the pass and into a narrow valley. Ignoring the fretting horses, she whipped them into a run. The sky grew darker. The bulk of the Shataiki swarm was almost over them. Darsal smashed into a winged serpent shrine and sent the idol and the incense altar clattering down the hillside.

Marak finally quit trying to get the reins from her and hung onto the saddle horn. "Darsal, if you'd stop for just a—"

The sand turned to mud and worn rocks. Darsal barely avoided a tree, then darted around two more. On they fled, zigzagging through the treacherous terrain.

Darsal stopped and dismounted. Marak jumped down and grabbed her shoulder. Her skin was hot and slick. "What's going on?"

"I know you're mad at me, Marak," she panted. "And you're going to—going to hate me for this, but I—I have no choice!"

"No choice but—"

Darsal whipped out a dagger and cracked him across the skull.

DARSAL CAUGHT MARAK AROUND THE CHEST AND UNDER HIS arms. She half carried, half dragged him over the sand. Her arms were killing her. Sweat poured down her skin. Marak's dead weight slowed her down. Darsal dragged him by the armpits to the red pool and plopped him next to it. She sank down along-side him.

He wouldn't be out long.

She caught her breath, then tugged Marak's head so that he hung over the edge of the pool. Darsal grabbed a tuft of hair and shoved his whole head facedown into the pool and held him under. She yanked him back out, then under again.

Marak started to sputter and struggle. Darsal knocked him out and jumped on his back. She straddled his shoulders and baptized him again.

Again.

Darsal plunged him back under, clinging to his scalp. She jerked his head out and shoved him all the way into the pool. Her stomach churned. She pulled herself over the edge and yanked his head above the surface by the hair. He was barely breathing.

Blood oozed out his nose and ran down his face.

She pushed him under again. "Drown already! For the love of Elyon, drown, you fool Scab! Drown already!" Again and again she forced him under.

Until he . . . went limp . . . in her grasp.

She dragged him out of the pool and rolled him over. A flash of light splashed over his skin. Her heart froze. Marak's flesh was still flaky. Scab.

Darsal's eyes widened. Her stomach curdled.

"No! Why are you still Scab? You drowned; you can't be—" She cut herself off as the revelation dawned.

It wasn't just drowning. Marak hadn't believed. And she'd drowned him.

Darsal ripped off his shirt and pounded on his chest.

"Wake up! Wake up! By Elyon, wake up!"

She slapped his face and struck him hard with both fists, slamming into his heart with all her strength.

"Marak, I love you. I didn't mean to hurt you!"

Darsal's fists struck the unconscious general's chest one more time. She raised her fists up, then let them drop. She knew it was over. Darsal fell across him, bawling like an infant, her arms around his neck.

"Elyon, Elyon, please . . ."

His heart. She couldn't hear his heart.

She sat over him. Stroked the scaly flesh and let her fingers hover along his torso a minute. She touched his cheek and wiped away her tears that fell on his face.

Once more. Just once more.

Darsal put her mouth to his and breathed into him, then pumped his chest. She breathed air into his lungs, then pumped again.

A third time she blew air into his lungs and prayed to Elyon they would fill and he would take in life.

Nothing.

Furious, she slapped him hard.

"Oh, come on, you stubborn, bullheaded Scab! If you won't live for me, won't you live to spite Sucrow, at least? Please, Marak, I need you. Why didn't you believe?"

A desperate thought passed through her crazed mind. It was stupid and foolish, and there was absolutely nothing in it. Something from another time, another world altogether, when a man had begged the Maker for the life of a boy.

Even so, Darsal put his arms on either side of him and straightened his legs. She lay directly on top of him, forehead to forehead. She kissed him on the lips. Begged Marak and Elyon one last time for some form of cooperation.

How long would it take for them to kill everyone? Days? Hours? Minutes?

This whole mission was doomed from the day I walked back into the dungeon. It's worse than the books, a thousand times worse. I'm sorry, Johnis. I couldn't stop either of you.

Darsal rolled away from Marak and curled into a ball.

"Marak," she wept. "Marak. My general. My friend. My love. I failed you. I'm so sorry. I'm sorry. By Elyon, I'm sorry . . ."

Darsal lay still in the darkness, the impossible hope that her general might rise from the dead forcing her to linger.

She didn't have the energy anymore. Twice she'd lost a lover, twice a man had brushed her cheek with a kiss, only to perish.

She didn't want this fight. Elyon had made her do it. The general had been so close, and then she'd ruined it.

Now she'd killed him.

"Elyon, why can't you just let me die? Take me, not him."

Mud stained her face, caking her eyes shut. She didn't care.

Marak was gone. Gone.

TWENTY-EIGHT

Darsal folded up on herself, limp. Minutes passed. And then, silently, languidly, a mist began to curl up from the ground, winding around her like so many octopus tentacles. Darsal twisted around, looking toward the pool where Marak's body lay. Already the mist was so heavy she couldn't see man or pool. The haze turned a purple-red hue.

Darsal got up on her knees and felt for any of Marak's daggers, even her own, stolen from Cassak.

Either the mist was too thick or she was too frantic to search. Helpless, worthless, useless, alone. She had nothing.

"Peace, Darsal." A musical voice floated from the trees.

Out stepped a delicate, willowy woman, almost glowing. She had flawless, white, translucent skin and wore a long, thin, green gown. White-gold hair fell to her calves. Her wide eyes burned in the darkness and cut through the haze.

The entity. Johnis's Leedhan.

Shaeda.

Darsal drew back at the woman's approach. Her mouth ran dry. The woman crouched in front of her and pressed her slender hand against Darsal's chest. Darsal's heart thrummed faster at the contact.

She couldn't pull her gaze from the woman's eyes. Her steady, penetrating gaze that probed the soul and soothed the mind.

That could seize control of body, mind, and soul.

"Peace." Shaeda blew a gentle puff of air in Darsal's face, an unnervingly sweet aroma. "I have need of you, albino . . ."

Darsal's body relaxed of its own accord. Her eyes drooped. "Who are you . . . ?"

Shaeda cupped Darsal's face and gave her something to drink from a stone bowl. "Take such."

She hesitated.

"Such is not fruit," Shaeda said. "Such will not yield you to me. I desire not to grant you my power, nor gain control over you. Accept my restraint."

Darsal wanted to resist, but found she couldn't. She obeyed, and the Leedhan removed the bowl. The drink smelled like Rhambutan and citrus.

"Shaeda . . . you tricked Johnis . . ."

"Men hear what they will."

"Marak . . ." Darsal's thoughts were scattering, petals breaking off of flowers and drifting away in the wind. "Johnis . . . Thomas . . ."

"Remain with me, daughter of men. The potion is strong, but will take time to work its course. Then such will enable you to resist me. Concern yourself not with this man. He is beyond your skill. Drink again."

The stone bowl returned to Darsal's mouth. She drank her fill while Shaeda talked.

"Johnis . . ."

"Teeleh's priest has the amulet, yet he must not keep such. The Shataiki must be thwarted, lest they kill every human in this world . . . and naught shall prevent such foul creatures from passing to the other side of the river. I shall reveal to you the way in which you must go. Comprehend you such? Daughter of men, awake."

Shaeda traced her sharp half claw of a nail over the scar on Darsal's cheek and down the side of her throat. She kissed her on the forehead and both cheeks. "Do not slumber now. We have need of you yet."

Darsal tensed, head clearing in the fog. "Johnis."

Shaeda nodded once. "He is shattered to pieces. The priest will unleash the Shataiki on your Circle. Your kind and the Horde shall perish. The priest will prevail unless Johnis dies. Do you comprehend?"

Darsal struggled to keep up. Shaeda spoke slowly but covered many subjects in the time it took most to process the first sentence. Time seemed almost irrelevant.

"Johnis . . . lives?"

Darsal's mind was reeling. Shaeda didn't want the priest to have control of the Shataiki. The Leedhan wanted Johnis and Silvie to drown. Needed them to drown.

My enemy's enemy . . .

"You want him to drown," Darsal said.

Pause. "You must make haste, daughter of men. Upon Johnis's death the amulet's power shall break. Retrieve the medallion and take such to the river. There you may cross but once."

Darsal bit her lip. "Why? What have you done to them?"

The maddening Leedhan simply could not answer quickly. "Johnis must drown that another might gain control. The son of Ramos refused me his whole heart; thus our ways have parted."

"You used him." Darsal scoffed. "You used him and left him for dead." But now her mind was catching up. Shaeda was not telling her to drown them out of the goodness of her heart. She was asking her because she was an albino.

Shaeda would use the very albino she wished to destroy to make sure Johnis was dead and her own plans furthered.

Whether or not Johnis returned to life as an albino destined to die was none of her concern.

Wench. Vampiress.

Darsal bristled. "How much time do I have?"

Shaeda answered in her own time. "The Dark Priest shall reach the summit at sunrise." She gave Darsal directions to Johnis's prison. "But a mile from Ba'al Bek lies one of the red lakes, a narrow oasis. Make haste and go there."

Darsal nodded. Shaeda helped her stand.

"But Marak . . ."

The Leedhan's brow creased. "Go now and be swift, daughter of men."

Shaeda took a step back, spread wide her arms, and threw her head skyward. She sang out a single note just barely audible. The sound permeated the ravine and shook the ground. Thunder clapped.

The pool bubbled. Fog swarmed around them. Shaeda bowed her head to her chest. And the mist was gone. As was Shaeda.

Darsal needed to leave. Her legs remained riveted, drawn instead to the Leedhan's presence. A rustling sound.

"Darsal?" The fluttering landed just beyond her. She blinked. All was dark save a pair of glowing green eyes illuminating white fur. Gabil.

The spell lifted. She shook her head, looked from Gabil to Marak's body lying by the pool. Darsal's jaw clenched as she fought the emotions welling up inside her.

The Roush hopped forward. "I don't imagine Elyon's through with you."

"How do I stop Sucrow, Gabil?" Her voice was flat. She rolled her shoulders back and knotted her fists.

"Sucrow? I thought perhaps you'd go after Johnis and Silvie."

"You told me to—"

"I told you nothing, daughter."

She tensed. "Can I trust her?"

"Trust her?" Gabil's eyes narrowed. "She is as determined as you to keep that accursed charm from the priest."

"And Marak?"

The Roush hesitated. "You've run out of time, child."

Elyon help them.

Darsal glanced up at the sky. "I need to move now."

"Yes, you do. You should already be gone. But a moment . . ." Gabil motioned her to him. She went down on one knee. The Roush touched his wing tips to her eyelids.

Darsal's vision shifted. She could see greens and reds and blues just as easily as the day. The colors were rich and dark, but she could see quite well. Her eyes widened.

Gabil nodded. Now that she could see him, he looked as if he'd been in a fight already. "There's your light." He smiled. "Remember, north."

Darsal hugged the Roush and jumped up. "Will I see you again?"

"Elyon knows. Now go!"

She ran.

TWENTY-NINE

Johnis hung helpless in his prison. The pit was deep and provided no comfort. He listened to Shataiki screaming into the night. Empty. Bitter ashes and stale vinegar. Johnis tried to vomit but had nothing in his stomach. In some ways he was glad Silvie was already dead.

Laughter.

"Your little female was a nuisance, a pebble in my shoe," Shaeda taunted. Her physical presence was gone, but she could still communicate over a great distance, and now she mocked him. Constantly.

"The priest is but a pawn in this. Still, he has pleased me more than you, my pet, who have shown weakness rather than strength."

Sucrow. The conniving, shrewd, lying jackal! If he had the strength to stand, he would climb out, run back, and tear the priest limb from limb. As it was . . . he couldn't ever remember if he was dreaming or if he really was trapped in a pit awaiting death.

Let them come. Silvie was dead. Middle was gone.

Sucrow had won.

"Do you truly wish to know truth, my pet?"

"Leave me," he growled.

The entity laughed. More infuriating, he still felt the pull of her eyes, the tug of her siren song in his head. He would do anything for her, even now.

Her purplish-red haze came over him. Johnis saw Ba'al Bek and the priest, saw the Horde conquered and the Circle destroyed. He saw the Shataiki enslaved to Shaeda, who stood on the precipice with her fists raised, amulet high.

Icy, invisible fingers slithered up his spine.

A scuffle came from above, shouts and flesh striking flesh. "How quaint," Warryn's voice taunted the intruder.

"Scared, Cyclops?" a semifamiliar female voice snarled. Metal rang out, and Johnis listened to the pair fight. Clumps of dirt fell on Johnis's head. He looked down.

The skirmish ended. A body thumped hard against the earth. Someone sent it flying down the shaft. Johnis turned his head away.

Warryn's one eye gaped up at him. Blood poured out his head and torso.

"As you shall be . . . "

Moments later the rope around his wrists tugged tight. A soft grunt. Johnis was pulled upward. His back and legs scraped along the side of the pit. He bent his head forward to keep from banging it around.

He submitted to the dragging and felt the final jerk of the line as he went over the lip. Then he was on his back. His tormenter hoisted him over one shoulder, rotten stench overwhelming.

Albino?

More deep, husky laughter. *"Such is at my disposal, my pet . . ."*

He refused to look, refused to let the albino see his face. The stale smell of overripe fruit struck him full force. Johnis gagged. Warm, smooth fingers touched his bared shoulder. He recoiled.

A cloth bag went over his head. The albino secured it and slung him sideways over a horse. He was tied across the horse's back and left alone.

They broke into a gallop, two sets of maddening horses' hooves bent on rattling him to death.

SHAEDA KNELT OVER THE GENERAL A LITTLE LONGER, stroking his face with her half talons. All was not lost, not yet. The albino girl was so overwrought with passion that she could not see the life slowly seeping back into her precious general.

Yet Shaeda had seen the slight flush of life return to his cheek. Poor wretches, both of them. It was best if the albino didn't know her magic had succeeded.

Piteous albino, to fall so easily.

All of these children of clay fell readily into her arms. She smiled, amused at her own scheming. Her pets never did learn. Pity the last had to perish.

But Shaeda needed this one, this mighty general, just as wretched a mortal as the smooth-skinned worm who destroyed him. Ah, Marak. So strong, so broken. Such was piteous, to lose so mighty a son of man as this. She half smiled and licked her fingers.

Overhead the cauldron lingered, and Derias's screams intensified. Such was to his peril. Such his reward for the abduction of her mate. Such the price the amulet guardian must pay for more glorious designs, designs such as hers.

An even costlier price would the great usurper Teeleh pay for banishing her and the other Leedhan across the river.

Soon they would all feel her wrath. Her calculations were impeccable, from the ensorcelled captain Cassak to the enticement of the female Darsal.

Such was pleasing.

And yet the tingling in her spine reminded her she dared not linger. Soon enough she would glory; she would triumph. When she brought on Teeleh's demise, all would be as they ought. She would rule with her mate, and rule well.

She took a lingering look at the general. Once she took her pet and entered him, she would know all of his thoughts at all times.

Shaeda leaned across Marak's still form and kissed him full on the mouth. A hunger overcame her. She clung tight and tasted his skin. Her needlelike fangs split his lip, and his blood tinged her tongue.

Reluctantly she pulled away, tracing her half claw across his lips, smiling. "An excellent lover would you have made, my general . . ."

Another of Derias's roars.

A hint of fear threatened her. Shaeda shoved this emotion back. He could not harm her, not yet. Not as long as the amulet's power held.

She rose up on her knee, slid Marak's daggers back into their thigh sheaths. Another thing the girl, in her foolishness, had missed. Shaeda then arranged his cloak and stood.

"Fear not, Guardian Derias," she said, half-smiling. "Your demise comes, and from there the demise of your master and all your kind." Shaeda withdrew a badaii and ate it, taking pleasure from the sweet nectar. "Arise, my new pet, my mighty Chosen One . . ."

THIRTY

Johnis waited in the silence broken only by the occasional whisper of a voice and the *bad-dum, bad-dum, bad-dum* of pounding hooves. He tried not to let his imagination run away with him.

The nightmares came anyway, as surely as the rising and falling slopes and the horse's steady, never-ending gait. The horse squealed and reared up.

Shaeda's eyes haunted him, her scent, her skin . . . her kisses.

Invisible talons stroked through his hair. *"Our time together was never more than a vapor, my pet . . ."*

I don't understand. Shaeda . . .

Someone screamed. The horse jerked back down, backed up quivering, readying for some great feat. Then it jumped—it seemed forever passed—and hit the other side of whatever obstacle it tried to clear, back leg catching the rim. Yellow, blue, and red stars sparked across his mind's eye.

Johnis cried out. The beast jerked, hopped, and fumbled forward. All grew still. Someone rushed over and checked the horse's leg. Another whisper. More rustling.

They were moving again, slower. The horse limped for a few minutes, then regained its confidence and strength. Its gait became steady, now slow enough that Johnis could feel its heaving, panting sides and hear its heart deep within its barrel torso. Foam oozed against Johnis's exposed skin. The beast was done. Its body quivered with fatigue, begging for rest.

Farther and farther from Shaeda, from his lovely, his entity, Johnis still felt the pain of separation, as though he were being torn in half by two powers. She'd used him, hadn't she?

And yet he wanted her. Needed her. *Shaeda, come. Come and save me! Come, and together we will . . .*

She *tsk*ed him like a child. *"No, my Johnisss, you shall indeed further my mission. You have accomplished my desires and brought the amulet to me. You have taken the Horde to the high place, taken control of the Shataiki . . . These you have done at my bidding. And now, now, my Chosen One, you must die. I have told you such, have I not?"*

You said nothing of dying!

"Your sacrifice shall not be forgotten, my pet. Yet your heart was never fully mine, therefore required I another, one stronger, one whose heart beats as one with mine . . ."

The stagnant breath of the desert gave way to cool, crisp air that smelled almost sweet. Not the sickly sweet smell of an albino, but a pleasant, spicy sweet he couldn't quite place. Like fruit trees or an intoxicatingly fragrant flower.

Crisp grass crushed beneath the horse's weary feet. A bird twittered, answered by what sounded like an owl. Soft wings and the faint sound of cicadas filled the silence.

I do not wish to die! Shaeda, no, don't do this! I promise I will not leave you!

She chuckled. *"Oh, but you must, my Johnis. My general cannot possess the amulet's power until the current possessor dies. And, thus, you must drown."*

His skin crawled. Twigs and leaves crunched beneath the horse's feet. They passed through a shadow. Water lapped against a shore close by. A few toads croaked in warning.

Rough, strong hands untied him from the beast and hauled him down over powerful shoulders. Citrus. Albino and citrus.

"I thought perhaps 'twas fitting you died at the hands of one of your former comrades in arms. She is going to drown you, my pet, and willingly. Her delusions are but misguided lies."

He was placed on the ground. The chain at his wrists snapped in half.

"What occurs when blood touches the water, my pet? Do you know?" Shaeda's dark laughter filled his head, making him dizzy. *"Such is defiled. And you have defiled that which is sacred."*

Someone sat on him and hammered a stake into the earth, pinning his chain through a link. Whoever it was jumped over him and staked his other arm the same way. The same treatment was given to his ankles.

His captor left him.

"Shaeda," Johnis groaned, writhing in agony from the cold separation. "Shaeda, my entity, my love . . . I gave you everything. Shaeda, don't leave."

More hammering, but several feet away.

A soft voice spoke in soothing tones to someone who thrashed. The brief conflict ended to the satisfaction of the first voice.

"Truly you are a fool, my pet, should you ever have entertained the thought I would share power. Nay, little Chosen One, entities do not share power. Yet I did enjoy your kisses and your embrace. Now comes my executioner, and she shall wish you to die. Fail me not, my pet."

Footsteps.

"LINGER, GENERAL . . ." A VOICE. A WOMAN. MARAK SHIFTED. A firm, slender hand pushed him back down. *"Yield . . . Fear me not . . ."*

He couldn't breathe. Someone was on top of him, lips pressed against his, breathing life back into him. Marak sputtered. Turned sideways. She held him.

Citrus. He smelled citrus. Darsal? No, the crazy albino had tried to kill him.

A purple haze flooded his mind. Marak sank back into the

dark dreams, hypnotized by a siren song he couldn't place. He was dying, dead. Maybe he would see Rona again . . .

Darkness.

"Awaken . . . mighty warrior."

A firm hand shook him awake. He reached for a knife. His eyes opened to mist, to a lithe woman with long, white-gold hair, who wore the fog as a robe. Her gown was green and bared her shoulders, scooped low. Her skin was translucent white and flawless, so pale he could see vibrant blue veins beneath. So perfect, so alluring . . .

His gaze met hers. She had one purple eye and one blue, both with thin, bloodred slivers. Marak's eyes widened. He started, but rose slowly, hypnotized by the all-consuming eyes that drank him like water. The knife slid from his fingers.

"Peace, mighty general." Her musical voice drew him to her. No, she hadn't spoken, not yet, not out loud. Her thoughts came directly into his mind.

They were in a ravine less than a mile from Ba'al Bek, next to a small pool. All was barren wasteland, brambles, and briars. Nothing survived this far into the desert—not here.

Marak drew a breath.

"Gaze upon me, O valiant one; think not of your darkened troubles. Rather, listen to me, and know that I am she who aids you . . ."

The woman ran her fingers across his chest, up his neck, along his jaw. Her hand closed around the Circle pendant at his throat.

For a moment she simply looked at it, a strange smile on her face. Then she let it rest against his chest.

"Who are you?" Marak stiffened. His hand touched the fallen knife, but he made no attempt to use it. He eased the weapon back into its sheath.

She smiled and withdrew a silver bowl he hadn't seen a minute ago. *"My name is Shaeda, mighty general of Qurong. Such I am who has brought you back from death's halls and to the realm of the living. Be at peace . . ."*

Josef's Leedhan. He never would have guessed such a strange creature could be so intoxicating.

Focus, brother. But the voice seemed weak, distant.

Shaeda's eyes seemed to grow larger, to swallow him up. They grew, and then he could see Sucrow on the mountain, preparing his sacrifice, preparing to use the amulet on the albinos. He could sense the Shataiki's fury, feel their rage and torment . . .

"Indeed, General Marak of Southern, of Middle, I am the Leedhan monarch of whom the Chosen One has spoken. Regrettably, his sacrifice was a necessary one. And now, now it is you who are chosen for appointed tasks . . . Drink, man of valor, for you are weak from your trials and from thirst, from this woman who twice now has sought your life."

His throat was parched, wasn't it? And how did Shaeda know Darsal had tried to kill him? What else had she seen?

He narrowed his eyes. "What do you want?"

She seemed hurt and spoke out loud for the first time. "Mighty warrior, I have returned your life to you. Assuredly, my desire is for your welfare. Shall you spurn a maid who rescues you, or disbelieve what your eyes behold?"

Darsal had said something similar. So had Jordan, so long ago. Shataiki, Roush, Teeleh . . . Why not a Leedhan? She had been trying to help them wipe out the albinos, hadn't she?

This was Shaeda's plan they were unfolding.

"Taste and see, mighty general." Musical laughter flooded his mind. *"You see, such is not so difficult . . . Taste and see for yourself, my handsome warrior king."*

He hesitated a moment longer, then accepted the water and drank. His head spun as the citrusy, spicy liquid flooded his mouth and burned down his throat. Greedily he drank to the bottom.

"What is that?" he asked.

Shaeda took back the bowl, which vanished. She smiled. Fog swirled around Marak's shoulders. She tickled his skin. "Such is eluweiss, made from herbs, teas, and the juice of the badaii. But drink is not all you require, magnificent one."

She then retrieved a purple fruit with translucent, almost glowing, skin. She took a small bite with needlelike teeth, then offered it to him.

He studied the fruit, heart racing.

"The priest has killed your commander and ensorcelled your captain," Shaeda said. Her voice was low, husky. She palmed the fruit. "He has crouched at the door of your victory, and his desire is for your blood."

Marak had partially extended his hand to take the fruit, but now he hesitated. Shaeda offered more than a mere fruit, more than food to sate his hunger.

"I offer you alliance," she said. "The Dark Priest has both the power of the amulet and the power of the Great One, whose name is Teeleh. I give you my own powers, my own craft. You shall have my mind, my eyes, and my strength coursing through your veins. Together we shall put an end to this one who would dare rise up against the lord Qurong and unseat his mighty general."

He stood slowly and took a step back. "You think me weak."

"This battle is not won by mortal strength, man of valor. You are strong and full of courage, and for this I come to you. Come, take the amulet from the priest and wield such against the earth's bane, this Circle. Then ride victorious to Qurong and be rewarded."

The gnawing in his stomach grew, along with the desire to destroy Sucrow. He heard Derias's howl. They were out of time.

Marak accepted the fruit and bit into the tender flesh. So sweet the taste, so forbidden . . . He held it there a moment, let the flavor burst over his tongue. His skin tingled; his head buzzed. His senses heightened, and Shaeda's power, her mind, her will, poured into him.

The smell of bats and humans, dust and Leedhan, assaulted his nostrils. The smell of rotten eggs mingled with the paste. He heard each individual roar, each flap of Shataiki wing, each nervous stamping of his warriors' horses. His clothes brushed against his flaking, morst-crusted skin.

He swallowed that one bite and felt it surge through him.

Shaeda's thoughts opened to him. He saw now how delicately she had orchestrated the entire scheme. Long had she considered such a plot, now coming to fruition. She had arranged Jordan's death; Johnis, Silvie, and Darsal separated . . . She'd left Johnis, who attempted to defy her, and now came to Marak, all with one purpose in mind.

Stop Sucrow and acquire the amulet from the guardian Derias.

"He cannot be allowed to wield such himself," Shaeda told him. *"We must retrieve the amulet, or else the son of Ramos's sacrifice is for naught."*

Anything to pay back that priest. He drew a sharp breath and devoured the remainder of the fruit. The fog surrounded them. Shaeda stepped closer, her mesmerizing gaze fixed on him. She traced his cheek and slid into his embrace, smiled. Her needlelike fingers tickled his skin. The heady sensation set him aflame.

"We have not time for the pleasantry of acquaintance, my pet."

Shaeda kissed him full on the mouth, bit his lip. Her grip tightened around him—so much strength in so delicate a creature. She wanted him, and he wanted her.

"My will is your will, my strength your strength," she thought to him. *"Relinquish all to me, my mighty warrior-king."*

Resistance was not an option. Not that he wanted it. He could eat and drink of her and never want again. One purpose, one mind . . .

Marak surrendered his will.

"Grant me your heart."

Shaeda's full might poured into him. His skin turned translucent: shimmering white and purple seeped from his eyes. Now he could see in the dark, invigorated by her sight. Rich, dark hues tinged purple.

All was not lost. This was only the beginning . . .

Marak sped up the side of the rock face and was over the lip before he realized he had moved. The wind against his face was breathtaking, exhilarating. He rushed northward, deeper under the wings of the Shataiki toward the plateau. Shaeda's mind kept him riveted solely on getting the amulet from Sucrow before he could use it, taking all power away from the priest . . .

Ba'al Bek . . . Ba'al Bek . . .

He had to reach Ba'al Bek, and he had to do it now. What he wouldn't give for a horse—although what horse could possibly run this fast?

Make haste, make haste . . .

His mind struggled to catch up. Shaeda was running at a maddening pace. She was driving him like cattle. Despite the shadows, Marak could see plainly everything before him. He could even make out individual bats amid the swarm.

"See and understand, General . . . Be at peace; go to Ba'al Bek and win back the amulet. Come with me, General. Fly to the high place . . . Make haste . . ."

"Why?" he asked.

"We shall overcome."

Shaeda spurred him on. They came down the next rise and into the canyon, then across open wilderness. There he saw a hundred warriors—Cassak's men—circled around the base of a high-rising plateau that fanned wide like a yawning mouth. The jagged piece of rock was easily over a mile wide. Their torches made a ring of fire darkened by heavy, curling black smoke. Oil and incense and burning wood filled the air.

The entity grew anxious beneath the Shataiki swarm. Cold fear trickled through Marak's body. Furious at her own weakness, Shaeda pushed him on. They had to get the amulet from Sucrow, and now.

No, not from Sucrow. They needed Josef to die first for the guardian to retake the amulet. Then Marak would take the medallion from the beast's claw and have favor. He drew a heavy breath.

Atop the plateau was another ring of torches, and from above he could hear Sucrow, savoring this moment and taking pause to worship his god before making his final invocation and calling down the Shataiki guardian queen on the albinos.

"High priest of the Great One am I, and upon my shoulders falls so excellent a task that I might be found worthy to speak words before the Throne and uplift my voice on high. O mighty Teeleh, hear my prayer and the invocation I speak this hour!"

Those words still made Marak's skin crawl, even though he must have heard Sucrow's daily prayers for years. Jordan's voice nagged at him.

"Tread lightly, brother . . ."

He pressed on. The men heard him coming and turned to look. Of course, they couldn't see him. Not from where he stood.

But the Shataiki could . . .

"Move!" Shaeda screamed through him. She lifted Marak's hand in clawlike fashion. The men fell away. "Stand aside!"

"Let the spirit of the Great One fall on me, for I have found favor in his hand!" Sucrow's voice continued to bellow across the desert. "Call down blessing and boon upon your servants; from the hands of Teeleh most almighty, the great one whom we serve, let goodness and favor fall. Rain upon us, O master of all!"

Marak plunged ahead, shouting for the warriors to get out of his way. He scaled the side of the plateau, Sucrow's opening rite growing louder with every footstep. A lightning storm broke out overhead.

He reached the top and stood behind a semicircle of serpent warriors in time to see a ball of light consume the Dark Priest. He was surrounded by two half-moons of serpent warriors, staff held high, and for a moment he glowed, his skin, hair, and clothing radiant.

Shaeda drove him into a crouch, bidding him linger still. The priest stood in the center of a craggy, rugged hole easily a mile wide. There in his black and purple robes, tight fists gripping the white staff of power, Sucrow truly did look every inch Teeleh's high priest and not a superstitious old wizard.

The opening orations continued—how long was the priest going to go on? Couldn't he just kill the bloody Circle and be done with them?

But that would work in their favor, wouldn't it?

In the back of his mind, a prickling sensation raised his neck hairs, and Jordan's faint voice drew his hand to his throat, touching the pendant. But Shaeda's siren song silenced his brother, directed his attention back to the priest.

"And may the accursed albinos fall, and with them whoever dares attempt to thwart us. Let their flesh shrivel and fall aside and their intestines rot and burst forth . . ."

The serpent warriors' spear butts struck the rock in unison and began pulsing like war drums.

Marak lunged for the priest, but Shaeda held him back. *"Patience, my general, patience . . ."*

But why? The priest had to die. The priest had to die before the ceremony ended and the invocation rang out. If they waited much longer, they would be too late.

"The Chosen One has not yet died. Yet, when he does, you shall attend the priest and claim the amulet for us."

You will kill him to further your own purposes? Marak felt a tingling in his spine. If she would turn her back on Josef, could she not do thc samc to him?

Shaeda's soothing hand caressed his skin. *"Have no fear, my pet. Such was necessary and regrettable. You, however, are required to live and rule with me . . ."*

Sucrow lowered his staff. "Bring the sacrifice and the blood." He took a silver dagger and readied himself while the serpent warriors prepared an offering on the rock, spilling the blood of the

Chosen One and of Qurong over grain and wine and the innards of a jackal.

The priest began to speak over those present. "A boon to him who hears my words, who this day comes to the mountain to glory in the work of the Great One, our lord and master Teeleh. Glorious and valiant is he who overcomes such evils and this day becomes participant in the destruction of his master's enemies! For long have we waged war against the diseased among us, those who would spill out our blood as drink offerings. Against such evil we have long toiled, and now, now, my fellows, my brethren in arms and in faith, comes the fruition of our labors . . ."

The Chosen One . . . The Chosen One was Josef . . . Johnis, onetime friend of Darsal, so long ago overdrawn and destroyed. Shaeda's mind opened, and he saw her with Johnis and Silvie in the desert, feasting with them as they succumbed to her power.

Shaeda's power, the mind-bending combination of speed, strength, sensation, and foresight that made her impossible to resist and so intimately desirable.

Johnis had to die, and once he was dead, they would take the amulet from Sucrow. But hadn't Sucrow killed him already?

No, not yet. Not yet, not yet, but why . . . ?

Not Sucrow, Derias. He hated Derias.

Shaeda's presence slithered around his throat and clamped down tight. Marak ached to be at the priest's throat, but the

Leedhan's talons drove hard into his back and shoulders, pinning him in place.

Above him the Shataiki hosts roiled, lusty for blood. They screeched above the thunder, beady red eyes glinting in the blinding flashes of lightning.

Derias, queen guardian of the amulet, swooped low over their heads, his massive leathery wings so close the tip nigh brushed Marak's ear. Shaeda tensed. Her fear trickled down his spine as melting ice. They both sucked a breath.

Marak's hand slid to his knife. Shaeda's intoxicating presence reprimanded him; his mind's eye saw the Leedhan's shape—her long, willowy body; her silky, white-gold hair; her perfect skin; and above all, her eyes.

And he also saw Sucrow in all his glory, bathed in a purple haze. Marak licked his lips as the startled priest resumed his ceremony.

A Throater placed a bloodstained knife on the stone before Sucrow. A row of seven Eramites, shackled hand and foot, was dragged before them. Forced to their knees, the rebel half-breeds were stripped, their flesh already torn and bloodied.

A sacrifice, as part of the ceremony leading up to the command to attack the albinos. The fool.

The Shataiki quivered and bristled with anticipation, all snapping their fangs and hissing at the victims. Sucrow stroked the amulet around his neck.

Marak drew his knife and started to rise. Shaeda forced him

back down, shoved his blade back into its sheath. Sucrow was so close . . .

Not yet.

First the Chosen One had to die. Marak licked his lips. Then the end would come.

THIRTY-ONE

Johnis tensed and squeezed his eyes shut. Someone knelt beside him—a horrible-smelling beast with a seductive voice. She untied the canvas sack around his head, then ripped it off.

"Are you prepared to die, my pet?" Shaeda's voice still taunted him.

He blinked, wrinkling his face while his eyes adjusted. Darkness lingered, with two million Shataiki overhead. Thin shafts of light flickered between black leather wings.

The same rough hand pushed his head and shoulders up a few inches and pressed a water bottle to his lips. Johnis turned his head, determined to resist.

"Johnis, don't fight me anymore."

Soft chuckling in his head. *"No, my little Chosen One, no longer shall you resist. You must lay down your life for me and die."*

He squinted and blinked a few more times, then turned his head to look at the woman beside him. His eyes widened, then narrowed. The voice.

Johnis growled. "Traitor."

"No, Johnis. Look at me. Open your eyes, my friend."

He obeyed.

"Darsal?" His throat was dry and parched. "D-Darsal . . . ?"

Her brown eyes were bright, brow creased with worry. Her tanned, smooth skin shone in the dusky light.

"Die, Johnis. You must die."

No, Shaeda, don't do this. Part of him still wanted his entity, his Leedhan. Her power, her strength . . .

Her will dug into him. Johnis squirmed. She really intended to kill him. And Darsal was helping.

Darsal smiled. "Yes, Johnis. Here, drink. I know you're thirsty. Look, Silvie's already had some."

Silvie.

His head cleared, heart ached.

You said she was dead!

"She shall be . . . just as you shall be, my Johnisss. She shall have part in your death. In this she shall serve me, she who would not give me your heart."

Darsal scooted aside so Johnis could see the second figure, much smaller, slimmer, and paler, also staked to the ground about four feet away. Just beyond arm's reach.

Silvie had turned her head to watch them.

"S-Silvie?" Johnis licked his lips, but his tongue was too dry to wet them. "I thought . . . They told me . . ."

Now he saw her tearstained cheeks. "I saw everything, Johnis. Everything. They made me watch."

Darsal pressed her water bottle to his mouth again. This time he accepted and drank greedily. Then he let his chin strike his chest. Darsal laid him back down. He tugged the chains.

"Where are . . . ?"

"An oasis in the northwest desert, a mile south of the high place. A particular Leedhan told me its existence."

"Shaeda." Johnis struggled, trying to clear his head as much as free himself. His blood grew chilly. The Leedhan was serious. She and Darsal and Silvie were all going to kill him. "So you believe me now."

"I believed you before. And I see how intoxicating she can be." Darsal's smile faded a little, mournful.

"What do you want with us?" He pulled at the chain. "They're going to set off the attack. The Shataiki, they're—"

"They've reached Ba'al Bek. It won't be long now." Darsal brushed mud and grime off his face and washed it with her head-scarf. Pain shone on her face.

"They'll find you too."

"Yes. They will . . . Sucrow meant to kill you, Johnis. If I wanted to betray you, I would have left you with him. Is that not right?"

She had a point.

"Shaeda told me how to find you, how to bring you here. And she told me there was only one way to keep Sucrow from using the amulet. I saw Gabil. He said she was telling the truth."

A cold feeling crept up Johnis's legs, then up to his midsection. Yes, he knew that too. Whoever took the amulet from the Shataiki guardian . . .

"You die."

Darsal offered him more water, then squeezed fruit on his wounds. The burning made him flinch.

"What are you—?"

"The only thing I can do, Johnis. It's a healing fruit. There's a whole grove here. Don't struggle. Now, listen. I'm trying to help you. So I need you to listen, and listen fast."

"Help us? We're staked to the ground in the middle of—"

"Just listen. Do you know why there is an oasis in the northwest desert, Johnis? Look to your right. Just look. What do you see?"

He turned his head and strained to see, knowing there was a body of water behind him.

A lake. A moderate-sized lake surrounded by trees with leaves as wide as Johnis's head, and long vines drooping down. Heavy mist lingered in the air, dissipating fast in the light of the rising orange-gold sun.

A red lake. The crazy albino slave had taken them to a red lake.

"By the Maker . . . you're going to drown us."

"Don't panic, Johnis. I haven't the time to calm you down.

But listen to me. I've thought about this." Darsal spoke quickly. "Johnis, Shaeda used you."

Johnis winced and tried to scratch an itch he couldn't reach. The grass made it worse. He twitched, desperate to make it stop. Shaeda chuckled in his head, voice low and intoxicating.

"My foolish little pet, heed my voice once more . . ."

Cold and darkness swarmed over him. Shaeda needed him free, free to kill Sucrow, free to take back the amulet and use it for his own designs. He needed her powers. Needed . . .

"No, my pet . . . die . . . Even your Elyon wishes such . . ."

"Let us go, and stop this nonsense. Sucrow—We have to get to Sucrow."

Darsal found the spot on his side and scratched it, scowling as she understood Johnis wasn't talking to her. When she withdrew her hand, it was covered with flakes of skin.

"Yes, we do." She brushed her fingers off and gave him more water. "Which is why you have to drown. Think about it, Johnis. Shaeda is half-Shataiki. She wanted you to kill the Circle *and* the Horde. She used you. Her power is a drug. And the amulet's power lasts four days or until the one who took the amulet dies."

The cold water cleared his head.

Darsal helped Silvie drink. She rubbed an itch on Silvie's arm for her.

"We can stop Sucrow. But first you have to drown. Both of you."

His mind reeled, desperate to keep up. Darsal was talking fast, and she couldn't seem to stop moving. Johnis scowled.

"Drown."

MARAK WATCHED THE DARK PRIEST FORCE EACH OF THE seven Eramites to their knees with Derias raging overhead. He struggled with Shaeda, tried reasoning with her. *Take it, take it now! Before Josef and his lover come back! Before Sucrow takes the amulet's power for himself!*

Shaeda wrapped herself around him like a robe and drew him into her seductive embrace. Her eyes drank him in, showed him what would befall. *"A little longer, my pet, a little longer. We must wait until the other dies. Only then, only then . . ."*

Understanding flowed from her mind into his, her answer to his barely conjured question. They could not take the amulet from the priest. Marak felt a cold chill at the next revelation: they would have to take it from the Shataiki guardian. From Derias.

His name brought bile into Shaeda's mouth.

She cut off the flow of thought and directed him once more to the crazed priest, drunk on his own asserted victory. Sucrow had not even noticed Marak here in the darkness, covered by whatever spell Shaeda cast over him.

From the shadows came a figure Marak hadn't noticed earlier but recognized now as Cassak, sword in hand.

Cassak was with the priest? *Focus.* Marak gripped his knife.

Shaeda spilled over him. So his favored captain thought him a traitor and sought ambition over friendship. Marak's jaw tensed. How long had they been in league together?

Everything started to make sense now. Sucrow had enchanted him. Cassak had changed sides.

"My general, unfortunately his eagerness to attend your family was not for your benefit. He used them, used your pain, for his own glory. Such was he who determined they would never be released. Qurong would have relented . . . for he as well lost a child to the albinos."

He felt an invisible knife tear into his gut. Cassak had him convinced he'd had no choice. But why had Cassak lied? He'd killed them on principle. He'd taken Jordan and Rona and Grandfather out into the desert and slaughtered them like . . .

The memory came back to him, stark and vivid as the day he'd gone with Cassak to do it. Thus far Marak had managed to silence it with Darsal, but now . . .

He drew his knife and started after the priest and his treacherous captain.

Shaeda's talons dragged him back. He snarled. *Let me go!*

Not yet, she insisted, not yet. Marak knew what was coming now, now that Sucrow took blood and sereken and poisons from deep within the desert's bowels and mixed them in a stone bowl, chanting.

Shaeda distracted him, setting his mind to Martyn's journal, so similar to this—minus the key component. Martyn had been thorough. From various hints and implications—either overlooked or ignored in favor of war—Marak had been able to glean what poisons would react with an albino's skin, what they would be susceptible to that a non-albino would not.

He'd read it in Martyn's journal, set his men to work making three copies of notes regarding the Desecration of the albinos. And he had watched as his family was eaten alive: their skin eroded away and stripped, their flesh boiled off their bones, their brittle gray skeletons turned to ash.

Nothing could spare them now.

Pay attention!

Shaeda tightened her grip on him. Marak watched as Cassak executed the Eramites. His stomach curdled. For some reason his mind drifted to his last execution. Jordan's screaming slammed into his head.

No. He never was, nor would he ever be, like his brother.

He was general to Qurong, trained by Martyn. And soon he would be greater than his lord.

Again the Leedhan cut off his thoughts, bound his emotions to hers. The albinos would die by Shataiki swarm, their bodies torn to shreds, leaving them to rot on the desert floor.

At last the final Eramite thumped lifeless to the ground.

"Have no fear, general mine, for the end shall not be the same for you. You will be great among men, for you shall take such and wield against all who oppose you. The time grows nigh . . ."

His attention centered on the priest, now surrounded by seven corpses along with his men. Sucrow took his knife and slit his own arm and mingled his blood into the mix of sacrificial elements.

"Blood of the Chosen One," Sucrow began. "Blood of the First and of the Ruler of men. Blood of the enemy, twicefold to die. Blood of the righteous, whose souls upward fly. Wine of the gods, elixir divine, grain of the earth, bound by mortal swine. Elements of air and water and fire; elements of earth, the living immortal mire."

Marak's hair rose, tickling his neck. His back and shoulders tensed. Once more his hand went for his knife. This was it. He had to act now. Already Derias was swooping, circling, lost in reverie and the anticipation of freedom.

"Not yet!" Shaeda screamed in his head. The sound echoed, deafening him. He missed the rest of Sucrow's opening, his final invocation. Shataiki wings thrummed. The end was in sight. Even Shaeda coiled up in anticipation, ready to spring at the last possible second. Sucrow continued his dark blessing.

The wind picked up, and the flames from the torches swelled, burning so hot and bright that no one could look at them. Sucrow shouted over the din, his voice escalating. Below them the earth began to rumble. A few Throaters lost their balance. Shaeda held Marak fast.

Sucrow's staff was high overhead, gripped between both rotting hands, knuckles white. His face shone in self-made glory, as though he'd seen a vision of Teeleh himself. Marak's heart thrummed.

The spears began to pound against the earth. Below a shout

went up, a chant from the warriors led by one of the commanders. "Death to the albinos! Slay them all! Find them from the four corners of the earth and cut them down! Let the sons of Tanis fall down dead, let them all be torn to shreds!"

Marak fought for breath. Was that him or Shaeda?

She cut off her thoughts and dug hard into his back with invisible claws. His nostrils flared. Time was growing short. So close, so close . . . Would Johnis die in time, or would she miss her final stroke?

Kill them. Kill them all.

Marak rushed forward and cut down two Throaters before Shaeda could stop him. He let out a scream that Shaeda cut short. The other Throaters turned, shocked to see him alive. He felt Shaeda dominating him, knew Sucrow was deliberately ignoring him, saw Cassak go for his sword . . .

"Patience!"

Sucrow's final rite began. Still Shaeda held Marak back, her hypnotic gaze his only restraint. Derias circled once and landed to the side. Cassak and the Throaters shrank back from the sight. The Shataiki queen stood waiting, wings unfurled, talons curled.

"And now, O guardian queen, blessed servant of the Great One, hear our emboldened request. For blood this day shall be spilled. A thousand years from now this day shall be remembered as the albinos' final hour, when the Shataiki came unleashed, and in their blessed fury rid us of this bane! Come, come to me, and ready yourselves; come to the high priest of man and beast, and let forth your blood-driven fangs!"

Marak and Shaeda both bristled.

Come on! Die already!

Shaeda's lip curled. Marak's curled. They both gave a low snarl. Marak could feel the end coming, the rush.

How will we know Johnis is dead?

Shaeda growled, frustrated with his questions. *"Such will not be questionable. Take heed and behold!"* Her grip tightened, as if checking the reins of a restless warhorse.

Their clothes flapped around their bodies; the great Shataiki throng hissed and snapped, whipped into a hurricane around them, their beating wings a deafening roar, adding to the thunder and lightning.

Sucrow chanted louder. Marak's pulse spiked. The priest put the amulet on the end of his staff and raised it high above his head. The roar above and below swelled.

And still Shaeda waited.

THIRTY-TWO

She really is trying to kill us." Silvie groaned.

"No, no, listen to me! So little time, so much to—" Darsal pulled at her hair and gave an exasperated cry. She drew a ragged breath and faced them, circling both of them. "Okay, you tried to bathe, didn't you?"

Lake water scalding his flesh, burning it off. He tried not to think about that. Besides, these waters were red, not green.

"It's been polluted," Silvie said. "It doesn't work. If you put us in there, we'll die."

"In the green lakes you had to bathe once a day, and the scabbing disease always came back if you didn't, right?"

"Darsal, don't make me go in the water." Johnis stared at her.

She couldn't be serious. She couldn't really mean to drown them. She couldn't really be conspiring with Shaeda to kill him.

"You've been with the Horde too long."

The pained look crossed her face again. "Maybe I have. It doesn't matter anymore."

"The gen—"

"Don't talk to me about the general! Don't talk to me about Marak."

Shaeda clamped down on him again, the moment of clarity lost. Her hypnotic eyes he could drown in . . . He had to die, for Shaeda. Could he do that? Did he want to?

He should leave the Leedhan to wallow in her own failure. Silvie was right—she was a self-absorbed seductress, and she'd used him.

No, that wasn't true. Shaeda loved him, wanted him.

And he wanted her.

"Now listen to me," Darsal said. "What if Elyon decided to make it so we didn't have to keep bathing? What if he decided to change something? What if the water changed so that instead of just coating our skins with water, we drown ourselves in it? Do you see?"

"I don't. Why would Elyon change the rules? And I am not touching that water. Nor am I going to die."

Shaeda . . .

"But you will, Johnis. The Shataiki can't be trusted. As soon as Sucrow uses them to kill the Guard, Derias will turn on him and kill the Horde too. You remember watching them feed off the bodies after battle."

Johnis was having difficulty breathing. He felt numb. Darsal was making sense. He just couldn't fathom the thought of getting in that water and inhaling it until the bubbles stopped.

"You're trying to kill us."

"Maybe." Darsal dropped to her knees between them. "Or maybe I think the only way for you to stop Sucrow is to drown. I drowned, Johnis. Do I look dead?"

Johnis didn't answer.

"Listen to me, Johnis. If nothing else, what's your heart telling you? Here."

His heart. Johnis groaned. He didn't know anymore. He wanted Shaeda, needed her. Hated her. Elyon help him, he wanted his entity back. The same one now determined to kill him at an albino's hand.

Fitting.

"This is about the heart." Darsal planted her index finger hard against the center of his chest. It hurt horribly. "This is about Elyon loving a Scab. He sent me to the Horde so I would love a Scab and love you." Pause. "Sucrow will kill you. And I might drown you." Her voice caught.

Johnis wondered what had happened with Marak.

"Johnis, Middle is dying. Sucrow is killing the Circle. Killing our families. Killing Thomas. Killing every human in this world. Decide."

"I'll do it." Silvie startled him. She pulled on her restraints. "For Elyon's sake, let me up! I'll do what you want. Just let me get up!"

Darsal hurried to comply. Silvie rubbed her wrists.

"Sil—"

"I would rather drown myself than let Sucrow near me!"

And Silvie dove in.

Shaeda laughed at a joke only she seemed to grasp.

"Silvie!" Johnis fought his chains. "Don't let her die, Darsal! Don't let her—"

"Trust me, Johnis. Trust Elyon." Darsal stood by the water's edge. Her breath was shallow, and she didn't move.

"I don't want to trust Elyon. I want Silvie to live! Let me up!"

"If I let you up, will you drown?"

"No! I'm going to jump in there and pull Silvie—"

"That lake's bigger and deeper than you think, Johnis. It's no pool, and you won't find Silvie. You'll find something, but it won't be Silvie. But you'll see her when you come out, I think."

Something. Something in the water.

Shaeda's eyes . . . beckoning him as she'd done before . . .

"You think!" Johnis started to weep. "Darsal, don't kill her. Don't kill Silvie. I'm sorry for everything. Just don't kill her."

"I'm not killing her, Johnis." Darsal released him from the stakes. He was on his feet before she grabbed him by the collar.

"Oh yes, my pet, go to your little female . . . and drown with her."

"Now, listen to me. You jump in there, you won't see Silvie. You have to trust Elyon or you *will drown* down there. You understand?"

He stared down into the water that still rippled from Silvie's plunge. The seconds ticked by. The impulse grew. Shaeda's will wrenched at his throat.

She was winning. Again. He couldn't find his heart when all three of them were ripping it apart.

Sweat collected on his forehead and down his neck and spine. Johnis tried to move forward, but Darsal had a vise grip on him and wouldn't relent. Seconds turned to minutes. Silvie hadn't yet surfaced. She was not going to die.

"All right, all right. You win."

Darsal stared at him, searching his eyes for a trick. He pushed her hand away and pulled off his shirt.

"You win."

THIRTY-THREE

Johnis plunged into the cold water after Silvie and swam deep beneath the surface, looking for her. The red water was clear, but he saw nothing. He swam in a large circle, hoping for a glimpse.

Was she already dead? Would her body sink or float if she was?

Deeper still.

More chuckling. Shaeda's laugh ran his blood cold. *"Perhaps . . ."* His Leedhan's haunting melody trickled through. *"Perhaps she is deceased, as you shall be. My foolish, troubled pet, so arrogant, so weak . . . If you must know the truth, then yes . . . I have planned such from the beginning, and you have all played your parts so well."*

You will not kill Silvie, he insisted within. That only amused Shaeda further.

If Silvie was down here, he would find her, even if he had to drag her up from the bottom. The farther beneath the surface he went, the warmer the water became. Johnis swam faster, listening for any sign of struggle, any gasping for air indicating she was caught.

"Shall I tell you what I will do, my pet? I have indeed taken another for my own, a new lover . . . one whose heart is fully devoted to my will, unlike you . . . you who always found me second to your troublesome female . . ."

The minutes ticked by. He was out of air in the bowels of the lake. He turned for the surface, but couldn't find his direction. He continued to swim, certain he was being pulled down, not up. And he couldn't find Silvie. Maybe the same suction had forced her under as well.

His lungs burned. Johnis kicked and thrashed, resisting the impulse to inhale. No, no! He would not die!

"Trust me, Johnis. Trust me."

He froze. That voice was not Shaeda. It was masculine, and didn't match that of the Leedhan at all.

And yet her laughter now came on the new voice's heels. *"Such will not be long now . . ."* Shaeda dragged him down, forcing him with the pull of her mesmerizing gaze, the lethal, bottomless eyes.

The surface was nowhere to be found. Yellow and red overtook his vision. He knew he was dying, thrashing in the lake like a fish caught in a net. The more he fought, the worse it became.

"Johnis . . ." came the new voice again.

The outline of a hand appeared, a large, calloused palm with worn and bleeding fingers, cracked from years of hard work. The hand extended toward him.

Instinctively he reached. Their hands touched. *"Breathe, Johnis. You need to breathe,"* the new voice commanded.

A sharp jerk pulled him down. Johnis gasped. Water poured into his lungs. He curled into a ball and started to sputter. Not like this. Anything but this. More water flooded his lungs.

"Breathe, Johnis!" the male voice shouted in his head. *"Trust in me!"*

The faster the stranger pulled him, the more water gushed into his body. His mouth opened wide against his will. Johnis pulled back.

"And now, my pet," Shaeda taunted. *"Your life is forfeit. Farewell, son of Ramos. Now, die."*

"Breathe!" the new voice commanded once more.

And he did.

Wide-eyed and terrified, with absolutely no way out and this hand pulling him deep, deep into the heart of the lake, Johnis stopped fighting and drew in a greedy mouthful of water.

The pain completely racked him. Johnis screamed and allowed himself to go limp, allowed this person to carry him where he willed. Everything went dark, and all he knew was the rushing water all around him.

His body was dead, he knew. And he knew whose hand he held. Through the darkness he went, boyish laughter all around.

Elyon?

The giggle swelled.

"Hello, Johnis. Swim with me."

Blackness gave way to green light, and green to red and gold. Elyon's laughter turned to screaming, and Johnis's whole body almost exploded at the sound of it, coming apart at the seams.

And then it ended, and they swam.

Johnis continued to breathe, taking in water in the same manner as a fish. They swam along the bottom and skimmed the mud with their fingers. Johnis quivered at the rush.

"There are still a few things for you to do, Johnis. Are you ready?"

They started for the surface.

Johnis felt the water cool, and in moments his head broke through. He flung droplets from his hair and swam to the ledge, then hoisted himself over, still shaking.

He vomited water.

A fair-skinned, slender body tackled him to the ground and rolled along the grass with him, arms locked around his neck.

"Johnis!" Silvie kissed him over and over.

Johnis returned the embrace and the kiss, savoring his reunion with his beloved. Then he stood, brushing himself off. He stared at his hands. His smooth, tanned hands. Even his injuries from the torture were gone.

"I thought you were . . . I thought . . ."

Silvie draped her arms around him and kissed his temple. Johnis looked up and saw Darsal watching them.

"Stubborn little scrapper," Darsal said.

The humor faded quickly. With one mind they glanced up at the shadow above.

Johnis glanced at Darsal. "How much time do we have?"

"Not much. Sucrow has already gone up. It won't be long. Now's a perfect time to put that brain of yours to use."

He ground his teeth and fell quiet for a second.

"I'm sorry for—"

"All's forgiven between us, scrapper. But we need to move."

Johnis studied the two women and looked once more at the brewing storm cloud of bats. Something else came to mind. In those last seconds Shaeda had said something about the general, about Marak.

He had to know. "Marak . . . ?"

"Don't ask me about Marak." Darsal looked away from him.

Like Billos. She didn't like to talk about it. And as far as Johnis knew, she still blamed herself and always would. A knot formed.

"Oh, Darsal. You loved him."

Silence. It was worse than the expected reaction.

"That's how I knew I couldn't force you to drown."

His eyes snapped open. But he said nothing. Instead, he settled his nerves and focused on the task. So Shaeda had lied. Marak was dead. It was only a taunt blowing in the wind.

"What of the amulet?" Silvie took the second horse. Johnis swung up behind her.

Darsal mounted. "Its power is broken."

MARAK STRUGGLED AGAINST SHAEDA, ANXIOUS TO KILL Sucrow and take the amulet, to kill the albinos and be done with it. She held him fast, invisible talons cutting into his marrow. He watched the priest raise staff and amulet high over his head, and a crack of lightning sounded behind him. From within the ring of fire, bats readied to fly, and Sucrow began to speak.

"And now, guardian of the Shataiki and all your brood, prepare to take flight! May your wrath take full vent upon our greatest enemy! Let all behold and be terror-struck, and all the—"

A sharp gale of wind snuffed out the torches, and a loud thunderclap shook the ground. The force of the gale was deafening. Sucrow, the Throaters, Cassak, and Marak were thrown hard off their feet. Marak landed on his shoulder and winced.

All went perfectly still. A tingling sensation took hold of him. For a full minute there was no sound, not even the rustling of wings.

They stood quietly, gaping. Marak saw the amulet lying on the ground, inches from Sucrow's hand. The priest rose and held it up, shaken but undeterred.

Marak's skin tingled. Purple haze washed over him. Shaeda's siren song turned to musical laughter. Her strength began to pour into him. His mind sharpened, homed in on the priest.

"And now," Sucrow said, his voice echoing in the strange quiet. "Now, go ye forth; hunt down and feast upon every last albino that has breath, from the eldest among them to the smallest squalling babe! And—"

A black blur swooped down over Sucrow's head with a deafening roar. Derias's talons slashed through the air and tore the amulet from the priest. The sound of snapping bone split the air. Sucrow screamed in pain, grabbing his arm, blood spilling from where the priest's hand used to be.

The Shataiki swooped again and threw the Dark Priest across the depression, then circled around, landing a short distance away with the amulet, Sucrow's bloody, ring-studded hand still attached, dangling from his claw.

Derias started to laugh, a low, dark sound. His wings opened wide. The monstrous Shataiki turned to Sucrow, who hadn't quite recovered from his fall. His large talon opened to finish off the priest.

Shaeda's restraining hand released Marak. Her power burst into him. Marak felt his skin and eyes fill with her unnatural light. He unslung his sword. Derias turned. Shaeda slashed off part of the Shataiki's claw and swept the medallion into Marak's hand before it could fall.

Derias bellowed, shaking the rocks. His huge wings pounded the air. Marak palmed the amulet and looked up. Once more the bats came alive, awaiting their new master. Sucrow shouted indignations and tied off his wrist. Marak vaguely heard the priest's healing incantation.

Shaeda's mind opened. She drove down on him. *"Now, my pet! Hesitate not!"*

Marak caught up. He bristled. Everything now hinged upon him, not the priest. But how . . . ?

"Johnis is dead; concern yourself not with him! All the power now lies with you, for you have taken the amulet from the Shataiki guardian. Use such!"

Killing the albinos meant killing Darsal. He couldn't—

"Well, what are you waiting for?" The priest snarled. He stood, still bloody. All eyes were on Marak, expecting him to give the incantation and command.

But . . .

Shaeda grilled him. Fog, purple haze, and searing anguish drove down on him, demanding he give in to such. One sentence and it would all be over. One sentence and it would be done.

Marak grimaced, buckling under the weight of her might. Teeleh's breath, she was strong. Her mesmerizing gaze took hold. Once the albinos were dead, he could kill the priest and take full control of the Horde, of the Shataiki.

Forever.

"Yield to me, my mighty one. Yield . . . Speak this command, and all shall be well; I wish not to harm you. But the incantation you must give . . ."

"No," he breathed, barely standing. He glimpsed Sucrow staggering for him. The bats had formed a ring around Marak so that no one could harm him. The cloud started to boil. Thunder struck the sky.

And in that same moment he understood the depths of Shaeda's cunning. She had missed no detail. A chill wound around him.

She had persuaded Josef to kill himself. Suicide.

"I can't kill my own—"

Her claws ripped into his back. Marak bellowed in pain, his voice ricocheting over the desert. *I will not fail!*

Marak ground his teeth. "I cannot—"

But he could, couldn't he? Destroy them all, purge this world of the beasts, these so-called men who destroyed everything he loved. Destroy the albinos with their filthy, diseased skin and their tyrant god. Destroy the priest and treacherous Cassak, those who plotted against and killed his family. Those who sought his ruin would perish with the very enemy they detested.

He could almost hear Jordan in his head, almost hear his brother telling him he deserved death, that justice demanded anyone who set themselves against the master should die.

This pleased Shaeda. Only Jordan would never want this.

Marak straightened and raised the amulet overhead before he realized what he was doing. One mind, one heart, one will, one strength.

"You have a new master now," he said slowly, savoring the moment. The priest would die first, of that he was certain. Marak sneered. "And now, hear and obey, dark servants of the Great One, of him who rules the brilliant side of the river. Listen and heed me, my puppets, my pets, for you in all your glory are about to face the ultimate defeat. Indeed . . . upon the destruction of these mortals of clay you shall fall from favor, and I shall rise—"

"Marak!"

THIRTY-FOUR

A male voice shouted over the throng, a rider rushing up the side of the plateau. No, three riders. Marak whipped his head around. He recognized Josef's voice but wouldn't have recognized his face if he hadn't called out. No, not Josef, the Scab, but Darsal's old friend . . . Johnis, she had called him. He had tanned, smooth albino skin and light brown hair and eyes. With one hand he held the reins; with the other he had a sword at chest level.

Arya charged behind him. Only this was Silvie—Marak's mind was still making the adjustment—with short, blonde hair and icy-blue eyes, two knives at each thigh and another ready in her hand.

And bringing up the rear—

His heart lodged in his throat. Darsal. Dear Teeleh, Darsal.

She brought her horse to a halt and for a moment just stared. Johnis and Silvie kept coming.

"Finish such and all is complete!"

"I thought you said they were dead!" he bellowed at her.

"They drowned."

Marak barely had time for that to sink in. The Leedhan's claws tore into his spine. A tingling sensation went up. Shaeda continued to grind against him. *"Recite the incantation; make haste and unleash these Shataiki upon the foe."*

"Marak, don't use the amulet!" Johnis shouted, reaching him. He circled on his mount, staying just out of reach. "You don't want to kill Darsal!"

His lip curled into a snarl.

The three albinos rushed across the high place. Darsal was catching up to Johnis, her face looking as stunned as he felt. Darsal had come back. She hadn't left. She hadn't—

"She attempted to slay you, my pet, my Chosen One. You are alive because I breathed life into your body and revived a lifeless corpse."

But the look on her face . . .

No. She'd left him for dead. He remembered the water filling his lungs, the searing pain as Darsal held him down . . .

Marak's grip tightened on the amulet.

"How are you alive?" Sucrow growled. A Throater had bandaged his arm. He went for his staff. "Get them!"

"You can't touch him!" Johnis snapped at the priest. To Marak,

"The more you rely on her power, the more control she has! Do you want to be her puppet forever?"

Marak bristled. "I am no one's puppet," he warned.

"He lies. Come now, brother, will you still not see your own illness?"

Realization hit. Shaeda had watched Darsal drown him.

"Ride with us." Silvie's blonde hair whipped against her face as she pulled her horse around. The nervous mount reared. She yanked the reins and steadied the animal, twirled her dagger.

"Look at yourself," Johnis argued. "Your skin turns colors, your eyes glow, and you aren't following your heart."

Follow his heart. He never had answered his own question: would his heart have killed his family, or died trying to save them?

A gentle nagging tugged at the back corner of his mind.

Shaeda tightened her grip.

Marak's eyes narrowed. Of course they would try to save their own skins. Shaeda curled his lip into a sneer and gave a low, dark growl.

"Marak." Darsal spoke for the first time. Immediately his mind refocused on her. She rode a sweat-slicked warhorse, armed and streaked with dirt and scratches.

"You—" He tensed. Shaeda clamped down, twisting his face into a scowl, forcing a dark haze over his eyes. The amulet. He had to use the amulet. "I should kill you all right here."

"You don't mean that," Darsal fired back. "You love me, Marak. And you always will."

Sharp talons drove into his skull, demanding his submission. Shaeda's song overwhelmed him. He had more reason to use it than to not. Marak ground his teeth.

"It's Shaeda," Johnis said, his voice stern. "Marak, it's Shaeda, not you."

"Joh—" Darsal started to speak, but Johnis raised his hand and cut her off.

He circled Marak again. "You've been deceived far longer than I, Marak. I know well how difficult she is to resist—and it's worse for you because you've been deceived longer. But she can't touch your heart, Marak, and she never will."

Shaeda's presence flooded his mind.

"Yes, I drowned!" Johnis snapped. "You cannot control Shaeda! She will use you and leave you for dead, just like she did me. We're alive because of Darsal, because Elyon sent her and we found him in the water, you understand?"

Marak could see nothing but the Leedhan's penetrating gaze, riddled purple-red, and the amulet in his palm.

"Marak, my love." Darsal jumped down in front of him. She reached out and touched Jordan's Circle pendant, still around his neck. He'd forgotten it. His mind centered on the sound of Darsal's voice, on her face, her eyes.

"Your mind is deceived, but you have my love," she said.

What does your heart tell you . . . ?

There was a commotion from behind, but Johnis and Silvie quickly put it down. Derias let out another roar, jerking against his invisible leash. Shaeda used the distraction to settle her mind and will into his.

Darsal ignored them, instead pressing her hand flat against Marak's chest. A dizzying sensation shot through him. Shaeda screamed in his head, but Darsal had him riveted.

"This is what I meant, Marak. This is what I meant." She kept eye contact. "Your mind is telling you to follow the Leedhan, to destroy everyone, to give in. But where is your heart, my general? I love you."

Shaeda snarled in his head. She would kill this albino harlot first. The Leedhan slammed full-force into him, sucker punching.

Marak's fist curled. He bent and fell away from Darsal, amulet still safe in his fist. He jerked back around, knife in hand.

Darsal swung onto her horse. "Come with me to the river, Marak!" She threw out her hand. "Come with me!"

His heart was not Shaeda's. His mind cleared, heart racing. The Throaters suddenly moved, swords drawn. Johnis shouted, back to back with Silvie. They pushed the Throaters back.

He could not kill Darsal.

"Get them!" Sucrow screeched.

They would die up here. Marak grabbed Darsal's hand and swung up behind her. Darsal kicked the heaving beast and sped across the top of the plateau after Johnis and Silvie, knocking aside the priest.

They jumped over the ledge and raced down the side of the plateau, past the mass of warriors led by Cassak. At the sound of attacking Throaters, the battlecry went up. Cassak screamed from above. Marak glanced back and saw his captain jump astride his horse and barrel after them.

Darsal threw Marak the reins and sprang from the saddle onto another mount, knocking off its rider. She slapped leather against flesh and raced on. "Come on, Marak, ride with me!"

"Loyalty, integrity, and honor," Shaeda hounded. *"Are these not your own words?"*

Darsal snatched his wrist.

Shaeda—Marak—grabbed at Darsal's throat with claw-like hands.

Johnis caught Marak by the tunic and yanked his face close. "We *are* completing the mission! Our mission is to put a stop to this, to keep the Circle alive. I swear on the books, I'm getting the amulet to the river and away from Sucrow—with or without your help! You are a general, Marak—a general under Qurong, the greatest of them all, in league with Martyn! Now, stop fighting the Leedhan with your mind and start thinking with your heart!"

Then Johnis was gone, Silvie and Darsal following.

Marak bellowed at the horse and spurred him after the albinos. Shaeda screamed in his head, the pull of her voice irresistible. He started to slow.

Darsal circled back. "To the river!"

He put the amulet around his neck next to Jordan's pendant and followed.

THIRTY-FIVE

Teeleh guided Sucrow's feet for three days as they crossed into the northeast and through a series of plateaus and mesas. The terrain was changing again, turning to quicksand and becoming a bold, fiery red.

Throaters and warriors sped over the rise and down the sharp ravine. Sucrow stood in his saddle with his staff raised high over his head. *Bloody fools they are, thinking they could lose anyone with two million Shataiki in their wake!* He felt Teeleh's power funnel through the staff and into him. A shaft of lightning broke out.

His senses sharpened. He could smell the Leedhan, smell the humans over the edge of the black, ashen ravine. The wind picked up. His skin prickled with excitement.

Cassak kept pace, his torch high. The wretched fire blazed between them, turned the ground the color of blood. Cassak signaled the men. The warriors split and fanned out into a broad semicircle. Sucrow rode ahead with his Throaters. Gradually they surrounded Marak and his albino pets, bent on trapping them.

The chase took them northeast, well beyond anything they'd charted. The ravine grew increasingly desolate, naught but a vacant wasteland. Here only the dead seemed to thrive—even cacti perished beneath the brazen sun swallowed by a Shataiki storm.

The air grew stagnant, repulsive. Sulfur filled their nostrils, mingled with blood and mire. Rotting flesh curled Sucrow's nose. The horses squealed and reared, balking at the stink of death. Sucrow urged the beasts on.

"Hold fast," he bellowed at the men.

Nervous horseflesh quivered beneath him. Sucrow licked his lips. All was silent and dark. The animals were desperate to stop, to turn back, stumbling with fatigue and soaking in their own foam. The ravaged beasts wouldn't survive the trip back.

Good. That meant no one could tuck tail and run.

Tens and twenties of men surrounded the ravine. Sucrow took the point position and rushed through the narrow valley. Hard-packed dirt thumped beneath their mounts' hooves. At this point not even the vultures circled.

They reached the plateau in time to see the blonde albino dart over it. They were gaining now. It was only a matter of time.

He sneered. Marak and the albinos would be dead within the hour.

THIRTY-SIX

The throng of bats seethed above. Hot, red sun vanished behind two million Shataiki. The bright torches from Sucrow's posse behind them looked like so many fallen stars beneath the canopy of black bodies and beady, red eyes. Darsal felt the horses pound against the hard-packed earth, already weary from their previous run, northbound over rugged, untouched wilderness Shaeda knew well.

All the while Marak had struggled with Shaeda, with the amulet. They fought and reasoned with him endlessly during the three-day chase. Barely avoided Cassak's three-pronged attack by using directions Gabil gave them to navigate a series of tunnels in a sprawling cave.

Darsal's night vision gave guidance through the tunnels and back out under the stark cloud that was the Shataiki swarm.

Derias swooped down and circled Marak the moment he stepped out of the cave. There the Shataiki spilled into a canyon fed by a black stream and overrun with briars and tumbleweed. Sucrow and Cassak came from opposite sides of the gap. Darsal led them in a sprint out of a winding, snakelike canyon into billowy dunes.

On they fled, Sucrow and his Throaters at their heels. All three albinos and Marak were starting to slump in the saddle.

The horses were exhausted and not going to make it much longer. Darsal felt her mount try to slow despite her urging. The poor beast had run from Middle to the Teardrop Canyon; back from the Teardrop to Ba'al Bek, which was well beyond Middle; and now to Elyon knows where.

"They've topped the ledge," Silvie announced. "Faster!"

Darsal's muscles momentarily went rigid. The long shadow of Shataiki drifted over their heads. All was dark and bleak, pain and death. The Shataiki queen, Derias, was up there somewhere. A chill snaked around Darsal like a noose and pulled tight.

A hot rain started to fall. Darsal smelled brimstone and ash. Death ruled this place.

Marak shook on the back of the horse in front of her, torn between two wills. His skin carried a glossy sheen and peeled away easily in the desert heat. His face was set, and he said very little. Every muscle in his body curled into tight knots.

"I gave you my love, Marak," she said as she rode alongside him, for probably the hundredth time since Ba'al Bek. "I give it to you still. And so does Elyon."

They headed through another canyon, trudging through sand that was gradually turning from red to deep purple. Crossing beneath another overhang, they left the canyon and rode and rode on. The river had to be close, in fact if she stilled her breathing she thought she might hear the sound of water even now.

Darsal glanced over her shoulder and saw the dust rising from the army behind. It all came down to this, she thought. They could go no faster and Sucrow was gaining. The end would come now. Dear Elyon, deliver us to safety. Bring us the river!

Then the river was there, looming suddenly as they raced around a bend. A red river. Darsal gazed at the other side and caught her breath.

There appeared to be no sun across the river. A dark, forboding landscape that looked like it might be hell itself! They'd come for this? Dear Elyon, help!

She spun back. Any minute Sucrow would catch them. They were trapped between the river and the Scabs.

"Hurry!" Johnis slid off his mount and dropped to the ground. His stiff legs collapsed, and he struggled back to his feet and brushed himself off.

Marak halted alongside and jumped down with Darsal. Silvie followed suit. The foursome stumbled forward and stopped at the water's edge.

The river was about fifty feet wide where they approached but widened both up- and downstream of them, stretching as far as the eye could see. The water was crimson from height to depth, bank to bank, length to length.

"Well . . ." Johnis stared at the water. "This is it. We have to cross."

Marak quivered, staring across the river. "Impossible. I'd rather fight here and die."

Dark, barren wasteland. A place for the dead. The mighty river was nothing more than a craggy red line that separated them from sulfur springs and the stink of rotten fish. Not even the carrion birds came this way. It was the back side of hell.

Sucrow was almost to them. All eyes went to Marak.

Darsal stepped closer to Marak. "Marak, please, for the love of Elyon . . ."

Marak stared at the water as if it were a thing from which to flee, as though to merely touch it might kill him.

"You have to drown," Johnis said. "It's the only way across and the only way to stop Sucrow."

Darsal tried to put her arms around him, but he withdrew. *I can't lose you, Marak.* "I can't do this again."

Johnis shed his cloak. He was going, of course. Going, and no one could stop him. Or maybe he was hoping Marak would jump in after him.

"We're out of time for arguing."

Marak wasn't answering. He stood trembling, grasping the medallion in his fist. His eyes were purple, his skin transluscent white, so thin Darsal could see his blue veins.

The Shataiki cloud had reached them above and formed a semicircle on this side of the river, spread all the way around the humans, boxing them in. She could see Derias now, crossing back and forth above them. The whole hive writhed in fury. Not one of them flew across the river, even the queen.

The bats were probably the only ones with any energy left in this chase.

Sucrow's Throaters pounded around the bend with Marak's warriors, now led by Cassak. They fanned out on either side and came to a stomping halt on worn mounts. Teeleh's priest trotted up the center, gloating in his victory already. Everything grew quiet as Sucrow savored his moment. He had them, could kill them at will.

Johnis, Darsal, and Silvie traded looks and stood facing the Throaters, backs to the river.

"Marak," Darsal said, loud.

Marak's expression changed. His face became dark, angry, full of something she'd seen only after the execution of his family.

"Remain, Priest," he growled. His eyes had gone fully purple, his voice husky and surreal. Shaeda. His eyes narrowed. He palmed the amulet.

A mirage of Shaeda appeared, white-gold hair streaming down. Mist surrounded her like a robe. "Toy not," she warned. The Throaters and warriors stepped back. She raised her hands over her head and let out the highest note Darsal had ever heard. The river surged, the ground quaked, and the horses spooked.

Darsal drew her sword and stepped to her general's right. Sucrow extended his remaining hand. "So that's how you want it." A starry-eyed serpent slithered around his neck, unnoticed by the priest. Darsal's eyes widened. She glanced at the others. Johnis and Silvie both saw.

The Shataiki queen suddenly swooped overhead. Derias came in low, straight for Shaeda. His talons slashed Shaeda's face. She remained silent.

Wounds opened on Marak's face, mimicking Shaeda's. She was still inside him, merely projecting an apparition. A flaming orb appeared in Sucrow's palm, and he hurled it at Marak. It slammed to the ground at his feet and turned to ash.

Shaeda chuckled. "Amusing," she taunted, gently wiping blood off her cheek. "The Great One sends his servant to deal with me."

"Marak," Darsal whispered. The Throaters tightened their circle on them, each armed with a curved silver sword.

"Contend, then, Dark Priest of the Usurper," Shaeda hissed.

Sucrow growled at her, snatching up his staff. His eyes turned dark and cold as he began his chant.

A low hum began, a thrumming sound that made the earth vibrate beneath their feet. Sucrow's sneer grew as the thrumming gave way to a chant in a tongue Darsal had never heard. She gripped her sword. *Come what may.*

In return, Shaeda began to sing, a beautiful, mournful siren's song that echoed through the air. It rose up, higher than the human ear could detect.

Sucrow countered with a low, snarling note. The sky grew darker, and the Shataiki above began to shriek and writhe in flight. A thick bolt of lightning split the air. The river began to boil.

Darsal's eyes darted back and forth from Sucrow invoking some sorcery to Marak trembling on the bank. She couldn't attack Shaeda for fear of hurting Marak. The pain in her head rang.

Sucrow's chant grew louder. To hear the priest actually pray was worse than hearing any of his other utterances. A death knell. His voice grated against her skin, raising the hairs on her body.

Marak snarled like a man possessed and flung himself at Shaeda.

HE KNEW IT WAS FOOLISH, BUT MARAK COULDN'T STAND himself a moment longer. He lunged, felt her presence bear down like a heavy rock inside his chest, and fell to his knees. Her laughter cackled through the air.

"Fear not, my pet. It will soon end."

He swayed, barely staying conscious. Everything crashed back on him, his family's deaths, Darsal, Cassak's betrayal . . .

They were all going to die here, by Shaeda's hand or by Sucrow's.

The water. The water could save them.

Sucrow laughed. "And what's in the heart of a man who tortured his own brother to death? Give it to me, Marak. You'll have total amnesty, and all will be over. We'll forget this . . . this lunacy in the desert."

The apparition of Shaeda stood in front of Marak, blocking him from the priest. Marak sucked a breath, set his jaw, and stood.

MAN AND BEAST WAITED ON THE BANKS, ANXIOUS TO SEE what the general would do. Darsal felt her body weaken.

Marak held the amulet in his fist and kissed it. For Elyon's sake, what was he waiting for? She groaned. Shaeda melted back into the general.

Marak was going to die.

"Servants of Teeleh," the general said softly. There was a quality about his voice that silenced the sky. The Shataiki grew still, and the color drained from Sucrow's face.

"Guardian of evil in this world," Marak continued, his voice stronger. Resolve clipped each word. "I hold in my hand the power of command and loyalty and servitude."

Darsal's heart sank. The general had made his choice. He chose Deception over Romance, Teeleh over Elyon. Knowing all that had happened, he spurned her still.

Oh, Elyon, how she had failed . . .

"And now, Derias, queen of Teeleh, listen to these words I say," Marak cried. "You . . . are under . . . my command! For what is done cannot be undone, that which is bent cannot be made straight. And after today the world will change."

It was true, Marak still had the amulet.

The general fell quiet a moment. He looked up, and his eyes met Sucrow's. "Kill the Dark Priest and his Throaters."

The air went still, perfectly silent.

Then Marak was moving. He grabbed Darsal in his arms, flung the amulet into the current, and dove straight off the sharp bank, plunging both of them into the depths of the river. The red water swallowed them both.

THIRTY-SEVEN

The water was so frigid it knocked the breath out of Marak. The Leedhan in him searched frantically for the medallion, propelling him downward, hand outstretched. He lost hold of Darsal in Shaeda's haste.

But not even she could bring it back. The amulet was gone, forever lost to the river. He'd lost everything.

Darsal swept past him and caught his wrist. She dove for the bottom, pulling him with her.

"No!" Shaeda screamed, tearing at his mind. *"No, no, no!"*

Darsal could not have had time to take a breath of air as he had. But she was pulling him deeper.

He shuddered, swam deeper. This was madness, all of it. Deeper, deeper he swam, unnerved by the sudden quiet.

"Perish, then! But know this: you can never return to the land of the purebloods . . ."

Shaeda let go. She vanished.

Darsal gave a tug, drawing him into the deeper, warmer water. Marak pulled back, lurching for the surface, desperate to breathe. He was trying to help her, not drown!

She was . . . breathing the water. Her chest rose and fell rhythmically. Demonstrating, she took a lusty gulp and swallowed. Her face showed no trace of longing, uncertainty, or desperation.

"Hello, Marak," whispered a soft voice. His eyes flew open. Who was that?

The seconds ticked by. Darsal treaded water, trying to stay with him, begging with her eyes. Her face grew uneven, rippling. Dark. The brown eyes widened. Darsal tugged at him.

His mind reeled. *Elyon?*

Darsal squeezed his hand. Marak felt his world going dark. Knew he was about to drown one way or another.

He steeled himself and sucked in a huge, greedy breath of water. His ribs and lungs and throat screeched in jagged, raw pain. Still, Marak continued.

All fell still and quiet. Blackness . . .

And Marak of Southern drowned.

But no sooner had the darkness swallowed him whole than a light blossomed in his mind, and he gasped with new life. His heart began to beat.

And his body shook with a new pleasure.

Life. Pure, living, breathing life.

"Swim with me," the voice whispered.

JOHNIS WATCHED IT ALL HAPPEN IN STUNNED SILENCE: First Marak's trembling opposition to Shaeda deep inside his mind, which Johnis knew all too well. Then Marak's order to Derias while the guardian queen was still under his control. Then Marak and Darsal diving into the river. The cold splash drove everything silent. Johnis couldn't breathe. For half a second no one moved.

A shadow fell across him. Johnis looked up. Derias whooshed over his head and landed to his left, so close Johnis could have reached out and touched his half-furled wing. A low chuckle rumbled from deep inside the Shataiki queen's chest. A chill swept through him.

Sucrow had his eyes firmly planted on the river, but he now turned and saw what they all saw. He went white with fear.

Derias licked his thin, pink lips. The priest stepped backward and caught his heel, but maintained his balance. He was ready to flee. But before he could even turn, Derias snarled. Then he was on Sucrow, ripping into his throat and tearing the priest limb from limb. Blood covered the Shataiki and pooled on the ground. Derias ripped Sucrow's back with his claws. Bones and cartilage snapped like twigs.

And it wasn't only Derias who had this thirst for blood. The Shataiki swarm suddenly descended on the Throaters, invigorated by their release.

"Silvie!" Johnis grabbed Silvie's hand and scrambled for the river.

Together they dove over the side of the steep bank into the cold, red water.

THIRTY-EIGHT

Darsal and Marak swam through the river, relishing the water as it rushed through their battered bodies. Marak's skin had become smooth and dark, healed by the power of Elyon's water. At last they reached the far bank and pulled themselves, dripping, from the water. For a moment neither was able to speak.

Everything had changed. The darkness was gone. It wasn't hell, it wasn't hell at all. Beyond the bank, trees filled a magical-looking forest, surrounded by color.

Then Darsal broke the silence, spitting up water. "You see?" Cough, chuckle. "What did I tell you? The Great Romance, as they say."

Marak stared at the forest like a boy struck by the wonder of a magic trick. He slowly faced her and his eyes softened, and he stepped closer. "I do see. I certainly do see," he said and kissed her gently on her lips. "The Great Romance."

The battle sounds raged behind them, but Darsal did not care. She understood more clearly now, her own love for Marak really was symbolic of the Great Romance. Of Elyon's love for them all.

Freed of any lingering restraint, she threw her arms around him, and suddenly they were falling into the shallows with a mighty splash. Laughing, they clambered to their feet and ran from the water onto the bank. Marak's black skin was clean and smooth, gleaming in the strange light that reflected off the water still clinging to him. Purplish-blue sand covered them.

The screams from the far side grew, and they turned to face the battle. Together they watched, breathless as the Shataiki queen tore the Dark Priest Sucrow to shreds and devoured him, licking his blood.

Johnis and Silvie . . . no sign. Did the Shataiki get them?

Cassak cut loose a shout across the river. "Run!"

An angry, dark cloud of Shataiki attacked the Horde who thundered back toward the relative safety of the valleys behind. Derias, covered in blood, roared.

Johnis and Silvie suddenly broke the surface of the water not ten feet from Darsal and Marak and splashed up onto the bank. "Thank Elyon . . ."

The battle across the river moved into the hills and vanished from sight. But the fate of most could not be in doubt. The distant shrieks slowly faded.

The four stood dripping, looking at each other like dumbfounded but quite happy children.

"Now what?" Silvie finally asked, glancing across the river. "We can't go back, can we?"

Marak gazed at the bloody carnage across the river. "Not now. Even if we could, not now."

"You will never return," a husky voice said from behind. As one they spun. Shaeda stood, watching them, her purple and blue eyes narrowed. She wore heavy mist as a robe. Blood dripped from Derias's claw mark. She was lucky not to have lost her whole head.

Darsal stood frozen, unable to break away from that siren's gaze. At first she wondered why the Leedhan didn't just tear into them and kill them. But then she knew why. The creature faced Elyon's power in them now. She couldn't climb into any of their minds unwelcomed, not as long as they had Elyon's water in them.

"For now, my pets, you prevail," Shaeda said. "For now." Then she turned, glided into the trees, and was gone.

CROSSING THE RIVER HAD OPENED THEIR EYES. FOR THE first time Darsal, Marak, Johnis, and Silvie took a long look at their new home. From the opposite shore everything had looked lifeless and evil.

But now a bright blue sun warmed them. The rich smell of citrus flooded Darsal's nostrils. No longer muddled with Horde scent, she could smell pine and ash, luna flowers and fruit. And other scents she couldn't name.

She stared at the wood into which Shaeda had disappeared. Rich blue grass and blue-black wood covered the hillside. Strange purple, pear-shaped fruits so translucent they almost glowed, dangled from a tree with broad, pale blue leaves. A thousand new smells and sights caught their senses. An insect made a whirring sound like a cicada, but not quite. Hundreds of small bugs flickered wisps of light. Green fireflies? No, they were shaped more like pixies, no bigger than Darsal's palm from head to toe. Nothing less than amazing in every way.

"Now what?" Silvie asked again.

Darsal turned back to the group and settled her gaze on Johnis. "So . . . let me get this straight. Shaeda takes advantage of your weakened state to control you. She gets you to retrieve the amulet. But she knew you would die and lose power over the amulet. She'd planned to enter Marak all along, as soon as you died."

"She couldn't have known for certain I would drown."

Darsal fell quiet. "She saw me try to drown Marak. She knew I wouldn't stop."

Her general squeezed her shoulder. They fell quiet a minute. From deep within the wood came a high voice singing, a siren's song of sorts.

"The world of the half-breeds," Johnis mused.

"Badaii," Silvie said, glancing at Johnis. He didn't respond.

"Badaii?"

"The fruit," Silvie explained.

Darsal scanned the edge of the blue forest. A cool wind tickled her skin.

"It's what Shaeda gave us," Johnis said finally.

Darsal searched their faces. "So what was her real purpose?"

"Shaeda wanted to take over Teeleh's half of the world," Johnis told her. "She's the eldest of all Leedhan—it's been eighteen years since Shataiki first mated with Horde to create the race of half-breeds. Teeleh kicked them out because they were half-human and he was jealous. Now she's back to exact her revenge."

"She needed a human to help her do it." Silvie's expression darkened a minute.

"She failed," Marak said stiffly.

"So be it," Johnis said. A strange look came over him, as if he were considering something new and grave. "So how did you two . . . ?"

Marak stiffened, but shook his head and threaded his fingers through Darsal's. She traced Jordan's pendant at Marak's throat. "I was captured and thrown into the dungeon, where I met Marak's brother, Jordan, an albino. He helped me escape and told me I had to drown, explained it all to me. When I came back for him, he was already gone. And Marak came in. Elyon told me to love the Horde. 'Return to the Horde and love them, Darsal. For me. For Johnis.' So I did. I asked Marak to make me his slave. Later he released me." Darsal glanced up at Marak.

"So Jordan was . . ."

"Jordan is with Elyon," Darsal said softly. Marak looked away.

"Oh."

For a moment there was nothing more to say on the matter. Johnis withdrew his single book of history and studied it. "We lost the other six," he said, stroking the soggy leather. "I kept it so that all seven couldn't be used to unlock the rules of history. With any luck, the other six will remain hidden until we can figure out how to get them back, but at least we have the one."

"Good." Darsal thought a minute. "Gabil said the books weren't meant for us. We were only meant to find them."

They all eyed her.

Darsal composed her thoughts carefully, trying to grasp the meaning that nibbled at her mind. "I just mean Elyon has different paths for all of us."

Johnis continued to study the book. "I'd really like to have seen Thomas again. He's safe, for now anyway. That's what counts." Pause. "You're right. We each have our own battles. Elyon didn't lead us to this side of the river by accident."

Johnis tucked the book back into his waistband. He faced the forest, eyes brightening with adventure. The old Johnis was back. "So . . ."

They stared at the magical blue forest with him. "So," Silvie replied.

"You ready to go?"

"What about Shaeda? The other Leedhan?"

A bird sang out from the trees. Music played deep within the forest, a sweet, light melody. Darsal glanced up. The forest really was gorgeous, a whole world of unexplored, untouched, and untamed territory ripe for the taking.

"We're protected by Elyon," Marak said, stepping forward. "I've never felt so full of power in my life." He stopped and faced them. "What's a few Leedhan now?"

Johnis grinned. "So, the end of one adventure . . ."

"And the beginning of a new one," Darsal said, winking at Marak. He returned it.

"The Lost Books are still lost, but we are now found," Johnis said. "I think that was the whole point, don't you?"

"To be found by Elyon," Silvie said.

As if on cue, the distant sound of a child's laughter whispered through the trees. Or was it just a bird?

"So then . . ." Johnis looked at each of them. "Now that Elyon's found us, let's see what he has in mind."

"Yes. Let's see," Silvie said. She put her hand in Johnis's. Darsal took Marak's, and together all four walked into the blue forest.

THE END

teddekker.com

DEKKER FANTASY

BOOKS OF HISTORY CHRONICLES

THE LOST BOOKS (YOUNG ADULT)

Chosen
Infidel
Renegade
Chaos
Lunatic (WITH KACI HILL)
Elyon (WITH KACI HILL)
The Lost Books Visual Edition

THE CIRCLE SERIES

Black
Red
White
Green
The Circle Series Visual Edition

THE PARADISE BOOKS

Showdown
Saint
Sinner

House (WITH FRANK PERETTI)

DEKKER MYSTERY

Immanuel's Veins
Kiss (WITH ERIN HEALY)
Burn (WITH ERIN HEALY)

THE HEAVEN TRILOGY

Heaven's Wager
When Heaven Weeps
Thunder of Heaven

The Martyr's Song

THE CALEB BOOKS

Blessed Child
A Man Called Blessed

DEKKER THRILLER

THR3E
Obsessed
Adam
Skin
Blink of an Eye